AFRAID TO LOVE AGAIN

AFRAID TO LOVE AGAIN

Joanne Lennox

Chivers Press • G.K. Hall & Co.
Bath, England   Thorndike, Maine USA

This Large Print edition is published by Chivers Press, England, and by G.K. Hall & Co., USA.

Published in 2001 in the U.K. by arrangement with the author.

Published in 2001 in the U.S. by arrangement with Dorian Literary Agency.

U.K. Hardcover ISBN 0-7540-4467-X (Chivers Large Print)
U.K. Softcover ISBN 0-7540-4468-8 (Camden Large Print)
U.S. Softcover ISBN 0-7838-9434-1 (Nightingale Series Edition)

The text of this Large Print edition is unabridged.
Other aspects of the book may vary from the original edition.

Set in 16 pt. New Times Roman.

Printed in Great Britain on acid-free paper.

British Library Cataloguing in Publication Data available

Library of Congress Cataloging-in-Publication Data

Lennox, Joanne.
    Afraid to love again / Joanne Lennox.
       p. cm.
    ISBN 0-7838-9434-1 (lg. print : sc : alk. paper)
    1. Large type books. I. Title.
    PR6062.E647 A69 2001
    823'.92—dc21   2001016690

CHAPTER ONE

'I'm afraid we're fully booked at the moment,' the receptionist said, and Chloë Vale's heart sank and she felt the first stirrings of despair.

At this rate she'd be spending the night sleeping on the beach.

'Well, how about taking me on as an employee? I can clean rooms or wait on tables. Are there any vacancies?'

The receptionist glanced at her doubtfully, casting her eyes down the length of Chloë's rather travel-worn figure.

'Hold on a moment. I'll just ask the manager.'

A few moments later the receptionist reappeared.

'I'm sorry. I'm afraid the manager says there are no vacancies at present. But I can take your name, and contact you if anything comes up.'

'No, thank you,' Chloë replied briskly. 'That won't be necessary.'

She needed a job now, not next month!

'Thanks for your help,' she added and before the woman could say anything else, Chloë picked up her bags and marched off through the same doorway she had seen the receptionist go through.

Chloë was slightly daunted to find herself in

1

the hotel bar, the air gently buzzing with conversation and the chink of glasses. The manager himself was nowhere to be seen. The bar was to her left, and behind it was the barman, tall and lean, smart and businesslike in dark trousers and a crisp white shirt and tie.

'Excuse me,' she said, dumping her bags on the floor.

'Yes?'

The man turned towards her, and for a moment Chloë's breath was taken clean away as she stared into sensual brown eyes and a square-jawed face framed by close-cropped mid-brown hair. She forced herself to get a grip. After all, it wasn't the barman she had come to see.

'What can I do for you?'

'Er, nothing, personally.'

Chloë decided honesty was the best policy.

She was about to go on when he said, 'Try me, I might be able to help.'

'Um, it's all right, thanks. Well, the thing is . . .'

Chloë came up to the bar, deciding she might as well confide in the barman.

'I'm looking for a job.'

The barman raised one of his dark eyebrows in dawning comprehension. Perhaps now he would fetch the manager for her.

'What sort of job?'

'It's not bar work I'm interested in, actually,' Chloë replied in an effort to be polite. 'Not in

2

particular.'

She didn't mind what she did, as long as it was a job. She tried her most appealing smile, the one she had used for particularly troublesome borrowers.

'Do you think you could possibly fetch the manager for me, please?'

The barman smiled at her, a lazy, charming smile. Chloë had to admit, once again, that he was good-looking.

'I don't think that'll be necessary.'

Chloë began to feel uneasy.

'I'm sorry,' she said quietly, uncomfortably aware of her shorter than usual skirt and newly blonde hair. 'But I really haven't got time to stand around and make small-talk.'

Who said that blondes had more fun? They probably got sick to death of men flirting with them all the time! Chloë wasn't normally the type to go in for sudden, dramatic make-overs, but then, the last eight or nine hours had been anything but normal. In fact, her world had been turned on its head ever since Sue had cornered her in the staffroom that morning and proceeded, in her calm, businesslike way, to destroy the very framework of Chloë's existence. Sue Pearson was her friend and fellow library assistant. Chloë had been unsuspecting when Sue approached her during their teabreak.

'Have you got a minute, Chloë?' she had asked, her face serious.

'Yes, of course,' Chloë nodded, somewhat bemused.

'Good,' Sue replied firmly, adding 'we need to talk. It's about Anthony.'

At the mention of his name, Chloë had felt a pang. She hadn't had many boyfriends before Anthony. Perhaps because she was an orphan she had always been happy with her own company. The job as library assistant suited her quietly assertive temperament, easy-going on the whole, yet she found herself able to deal with difficult borrowers when necessary.

Not that Anthony had been a difficult borrower. On the contrary, she had been intensely flattered when this handsome, charming young man had come into the library and asked her out. Chloë was unaware of her own attractiveness, oblivious to the appeal of long hair, slanting green eyes and a tall, slender figure. And she had been unable to believe it when, a few months later, Anthony proposed to her.

They had set a date, and the weeks had flown by. Now, it was only days to the wedding. Chloë had wanted to work right up to her wedding day, choosing to save all her precious annual leave for the honeymoon itself. Like any bride-to-be, she viewed the coming wedding with a mixture of excitement and apprehension. Yet, by the time Sue Pearson had finished saying what she had to say that fateful Thursday morning, Chloë had been sure of only one thing—that, knowing what she now did about her fiancé, there was no way she could go through with the wedding.

'I—I can't believe it,' she'd stammered.

'You're in shock, Chloë. It's only to be expected. Take the afternoon off, go home and think things through,' Sue had urged sympathetically.

'Thanks, Sue,' Chloë eventually managed to say. 'You're a real friend. But the thing is, I don't think I need to think things through. There's no way I can go ahead with the wedding now.'

'Are you sure you're not being too hasty?' Sue exclaimed.

'Yes, I'm sure,' Chloë replied firmly.

'So, what are you going to do?' Sue breathed.

'I've got to get out of here, get away,' Chloë said, desperately casting about in her mind. 'Could you tell Eileen I'm going? And Jen and Alison? Say I might be away for some time?'

Eileen was the head librarian and wasn't in that day.

Back at her tiny flat, Chloë wasted no time. She got to work, flinging possessions haphazardly into her small suitcases, the suitcase she had already started packing for the honeymoon. She worked with trembling fingers, terrified that at any moment she would be discovered. Eventually the packing was finished, and, after checking the train times,

5

Chloë took one last look around the poky, rented rooms before coiling up her hair and shoving an old baseball cap on to her head as some meagre means of disguise, then grabbing her small case and fleeing.

Chloë moved around the town's crowded shopping streets like a haunted animal. After queuing for what seemed like an age, she cleared out her bank and building society accounts, the modest amount of cash nestling in the purse within her handbag. She had to run for the train, but caught it with seconds to spare, and was aware of a sense of exhilaration as she sank back in the seat and the train pulled out of the station.

A ticket for the West Country, Wareham to be precise, was tucked into her handbag. She'd always fancied a holiday there and it seemed a safe distance away from Southbridge. Maybe the next day she would move on.

It seemed no time at all before the train pulled into Southampton, where she had to change trains. The large town's shopping streets proved ideal for her whirlwind tour of the fashion boutiques. It felt strange discarding her beige raincoat, long, flowing brown skirt and cream blouse in the changing room, and putting on the fitted skirts and smart tops she had selected, clothes that no-one she knew would ever recognise her in.

Gazing at her reflection in the changing-room mirror, Chloë could scarcely believe it was her, the tall, young woman with the shapely figure and long, slender legs. There was only one note that jarred, the silky, shoulder-length dark hair.

Back on the train, Chloë pulled down the window, slid the engagement ring off her finger and flung it out into the darkening night. As she closed the window, she felt a sense of liberation. Settling back in her seat, she flicked open the pages of a glossy magazine, the sort of magazine she normally wouldn't dream of buying.

'Excuse me, is this seat taken?'

Chloë almost jumped out of her skin.

'Er—no,' she stammered.

The train was pulling out of Poole station, only a few stops away from her destination.

'Where are you headed?' the woman asked with a friendly smile, once she had settled two of her children in the seat opposite, holding the youngest on her lap.

'Oh, er, Wareham.'

Chloë was startled into telling the truth.

'Same here. Then we get the bus the rest of the way back to Ecclesdon.'

Chloë knew she should have been wary, but there was something reassuring about the woman with her kind brown eyes and easy smile, her soft voice with the lilting Dorset accent.

'Just been in Poole buying the kids' school uniforms for next term. It's amazing how quickly they grow out of things. My name's Mary, by the way,' the woman added and offered a hand. 'Mary Field.'

'Chloë Vale,' Chloë heard herself responding automatically, before the woman lapsed back into her easy chat, for the rest of the short journey.

'Must dash.'

Mary was already getting herself and the children to their feet as the train pulled into Wareham station.

'Only the connection's sometimes a bit tight. Nice to meet you. 'Bye.'

And before Chloë could answer, she was gone in a flurry of children and bags. Chloë hesitated for a moment, before disembarking from the train and following the signs to the town centre. It was nearly closing time, but maybe if she was quick there was time to do something about her hair. She dashed into the first hairdresser's she came across.

Chloë sat and gazed at herself in the hairdresser's mirror and heard herself saying recklessly to the stylist, 'I want something completely different.'

She pointed to a photo of a short blonde style, swept back at the sides that seemed to accentuate the model's eyes and high, slanting cheekbones.

'Are you sure?' the woman asked doubtfully. 'Only, it seems such a drastic change.'

'I don't know,' Chloë hesitated. 'The thing

is, you see, I wanted a completely different look.'

The woman nodded understandingly, and after a few moments more discussion, got to work.

The finished result suited Chloë surprisingly well.

'I look just like the picture,' she breathed.

The change of style revealed cheekbones Chloë hadn't even known she possessed, and the new, dazzling blonde style brought out the emerald green of her eyes. She paid the bill and tipped the hairdresser generously.

Just as she reached the bus-stop the bus pulled in, and she read the destination on its front—Ecclesdon. The same place Mary Field had been heading for. As the vehicle rolled along, through countryside half-visible but still stunning in the growing darkness, Chloë wondered what had led her to follow a woman she barely knew, to a place she hadn't intended going. Perhaps, she reasoned, it was Fate.

When the bus pulled up outside the station in the seaside town of Ecclesdon, Chloë headed for the seafront, hoping to find a cheap hotel or bed and breakfast for the night. But she hadn't banked on the fact that it was July, well into the tourist season, and the first three hotels she tried were fully booked.

By now she was heading towards the east of the town, where the hotels looked larger and plusher. Gathering all her courage as well as her bags together, Chloë had mounted the steps of the Hotel Collingwood. And so here she was, trying to get hold of the manager so that she could somehow persuade him into giving her a job. It was just her luck to be stuck with this smart alec of a barman.

'Look,' she went on, 'I appreciate it's part of your job to make conversation with the clientèle, but I haven't just popped in for a leisurely drink. My time is of the essence, and I really can't afford to waste it.'

'I can assure you my time's just as valuable as yours,' the barman said coolly, as if he was fully aware of what she was implying.

Chloë flushed, embarrassed and confused. How could she have so misread the signals he was sending out? From the expression on his face now, it was almost as if he despised her. But then who was he to look down on her? He was only a barman.

'Actually,' the man went on, 'the reason it won't be necessary for me to fetch the manager, is because he's here now.'

'Oh? Where?'

Chloë looked eagerly around for the returning manager.

'You're looking at him. I'm just holding the fort, actually, until the barman gets back.'

'What?' Chloë was speechless. 'You're the manager?'

'Why not? Don't I look professional

enough?'

He came out from behind the bar and picked a dark jacket up from the bar stool next to her, shrugging himself into it.

'Is that better?'

As the man turned to face her, the full enormity of Chloë's mistake hit her. The jacket transformed him from a rather-too-smart barman into a slick-looking, sharp-suited businessman. It threw his face into new relief, too, a handsome face, as she had already noted, but one on which ruthlessness and determination were unmistakably etched. Only the faint laughter lines around his eyes and mouth softened the image.

'So, here I am, Dominic Ryan, manager of the Hotel Collingwood,' he introduced himself, offering a large hand which Chloë shook reluctantly. 'What can I do for you?'

'Oh—er, I—'

'Cheers, Dom.'

At that moment a balding, avuncular figure returned to his post.

'So this is the—'

Dominic Ryan nodded as Chloë's sentence trailed off. She had to suppress a smile at the thought that she had got the two men confused.

'No problem, Joe,' the manager responded to the barman, then turned back to Chloë. 'Well?'

Taking a deep breath, Chloë recovered

11

herself.

'Well, I was wondering if you had any vacancies.'

The man frowned.

'You're the one who was asking earlier, aren't you? I thought I told Linda to tell you we don't need any more staff at the moment.'

'I know,' she replied determinedly, 'but I thought—well, I thought it might be better if I spoke to you in person.'

'Really?'

He raised an ironic eyebrow, brown eyes sizing Chloë up. She felt uneasy in the unaccustomed clothes. It wasn't really herself she was presenting to the outside world. She was masquerading as someone else. Could she cope with the effects?

'And what,' the man went on, his tone faintly mocking, 'did you think I would find so persuasive about you, once I saw you in the flesh?'

Chloë blushed.

'I wouldn't demean either of us by assuming I could sweet-talk you into hiring me.'

'Sweet-talk?' he interrupted. 'I doubt if you're capable of such a thing.'

'I just thought,' Chloë ploughed on, 'if I informed you myself of my relevant skills, you might decide that employing me was too good an opportunity to miss.'

For a split-second, amusement glowed in the brown eyes.

'One minute you're all but insulting me, the next you're going all out to impress me. You certainly don't lack in confidence, Miss—er—'

'Johnson. Chloë Johnson,' Chloë replied, thinking quickly.

She regretted now telling Mary Field her real name, but hopefully she would never see her again.

'Haven't you ever heard of the phrase blowing your own trumpet?'

'I don't see what's wrung with a little self-publicity,' Chloë replied evenly. 'Especially when it's justified.'

Good heavens! What had got into her? These new clothes and hairstyle must be going to her head. She never normally said things like that. But she probably usually played down her good points too much.

'So, Miss Johnson,' the man rejoined, 'what are these relevant skills you are so anxious for me to know about?'

That was a good question. Of course, she had never waitressed or cleaned rooms in her life before.

'I'm a good worker,' she answered, plumping for honesty. 'I'm conscientious and reliable, and I'll turn my hand to anything.'

'I'm sorry. Miss Johnson. Like I said before, we really haven't got any vacancies at present.'

Suddenly Chloë was full of indignant anger. Why had he kept her so long when he obviously never had any intention of offering

13

her a job?

'I'll be off, then.'

She fought to keep her voice civil as she gathered her bags together.

'I'll try and find a room for the night before all the hotels and bed and breakfasts have shut their doors.'

'Miss Johnson,' the manager called her back, 'I'm sure we can find you a room for the night.'

But Chloë had no intention of letting him salve his conscience by providing her with a room.

'No, thanks,' she said quietly, adding under her breath, 'I wouldn't stay here if you paid me.'

When she had gone, the barman, Joe, who had been watching their exchange with interest, turned to Dominic Ryan.

'Shame you didn't have any vacancies, Dom. She was a nice-looking young lady, and she had a bit of spirit, too. Maybe you've just passed up a good business opportunity,' Joe persisted. 'What about Steve? You said if he didn't turn up again tomorrow you'd give him the sack. You could've offered your Miss Johnson his job. I bet she meant it when she said she was a good worker.'

'She's not my Miss Johnson,' Dominic said irritably. 'Still, I suppose you're right. Miss Johnson did have her redeeming qualities.'

Joe Chambers winked, nudging his friend

14

and employer.

'Redeeming qualities? So you did notice she had a pretty face.'

Dominic sighed. Normally he enjoyed Joe's banter, but it had been a particularly long, hard day, and he was tired.

'She's not my type,' he replied, remembering the admittedly attractive face framed by striking blonde hair. 'I prefer the more natural look.'

But somehow, though he tried to dismiss Chloë Johnson from his mind, he was haunted by intense eyes that seemed strangely incongruous with the rest of that attractive, yet superficial persona.

When Chloë's portable alarm clock woke her at six the next morning, she felt an overwhelming urge to switch off the alarm, turn over and go back to sleep. But suddenly she was struck by the unfamiliarity of her surroundings, and opened her eyes wider, staring anxiously at the small bed and breakfast room around her.

Then it all came flooding back, the events of the long, long previous day, her conversation with Sue and the flight to Dorset. Her heart began to pound as she struggled up on the pink nylon-covered pillows. She half expected to hear Anthony hammering on the door. After all, she thought, her heart lurching ominously, tomorrow was supposed to be her wedding day.

It was only after she had showered and was about to dress that she realised she was missing her carrier bag full of new outfits. Mentally Chloë retraced yesterday's steps before realising, with sinking heart, that she must have left it in the bar of the Hotel Collingwood. She didn't remember having it when she eventually found this small bed and breakfast. Never mind, she would pop in and collect it straight after breakfast.

Then she would get down to the station and catch the first train out of here. She would just have to go farther afield to continue the serious business of looking for accommodation, and a job.

'Yes, we've got your bag,' the receptionist told Chloë an hour or so later. 'I'll jut pop out the back and get it.'

'Great, thanks.'

While she was waiting, Chloë idly scanned one of the leaflets on the reception desk, advertising some of the local area's attractions. A moment later she was caught off-guard by a familiar voice saying, 'Here's your bag, Miss Johnson.'

Standing before her was none other than Mr Ryan, the manager.

'Thank you,' Chloë said, holding out her hand in anticipation.

But Dominic Ryan didn't hand her the bag. Instead he said, 'Could I have a word with you for a moment, Miss Johnson. If you'd like to

16

follow me through to the office.'

Chloë was about to say that, no, she would not like to follow him through to the office, but he had already disappeared with her bag, through the door behind Reception. In the small office he closed the door behind her. He indicated a seat for her and then sat down himself.

'What do you want, Mr Ryan?' Chloë asked. 'To waste more of my time, keeping me hanging on in the false hope that you might just give me a job?'

'Look, Miss Johnson, Chloë,' he replied, 'if I did have a job vacancy, the people I employ not only have to be good, reliable workers, they also need an ability to get on with people, especially the guests. I can't have staff who fly off the handle at the slightest provocation.'

'There you go again!' she interrupted him indignantly. 'You never had any intention of offering me a job, not after I condemned myself by my initial faux-pas, before we even began to talk business. Why couldn't you have told me as much from the start,' she went on, her normally quiet voice rising with emotion, 'before I demeaned myself by virtually grovelling for a job?'

To her chagrin, the corners of the man's mouth curled with amusement.

'There's nothing demeaning about needing a job, Chloë.'

'This is all just a big joke to you, isn't it?'

Chloë seethed. 'You've been toying with me from the word go, letting me believe you were the barman last night, when you could easily have told me you were the manager.'

'I might have done,' Dominic interjected smoothly, 'if I could have got a word in edgeways.'

'Well, you don't seem to have any trouble interrupting me now.'

Chloë's voice had risen several indignant decibels and she suspected that guests at the reception would be able to hear her through the thin wall, but she didn't care.

'So I take it you're going to decline my offer of a job?'

The words came so out of the blue, that Chloë didn't believe her ears.

'What?'

'You heard what I said.'

'If you're joking again,' Chloë began suspiciously.

'I never joke about business,' Dominic stated with quiet firmness.

'I can believe that.'

'What?' Dominic Ryan asked sternly.

'Nothing,' she replied quickly. 'Of course I'd love a job,' she gushed.

'Well, a waitressing job's yours if you want it, plus lodgings, of course.'

'Oh! Thank you! But I thought I'd blown it.'

Dominic Ryan shrugged.

'I changed my mind.'

'Changed your mind? Why?'

'Well,' he admitted grudgingly, 'another member of staff has let me down. It's peak season, and we need a full complement of staff. Besides,' he went on, 'I like someone who can hold their own. It's a tough job being a waitress. You need to be able to deal with all types of customer, without offending them of course.'

'Oh, I see.'

The fact that he was offering her a job finally sank in, and delight sprang in Chloë's heart.

'Thank you, that's marvellous, Mr Ryan. You won't regret it. Try me for a week, and if you're not satisfied by then, you can throw me out on my ear.'

'I might hold you to that,' Mr Ryan replied, the hardness having returned to his face.

'So, when do you want me to start?' Chloë asked brightly. 'Now?'

Suddenly brisk and businesslike, Dominic Ryan strode over to the large work rota on the wall.

'We've got a temp in for the day now, and it looks as though we're OK for tomorrow morning. But you can start tomorrow evening. Report to the kitchens at six-thirty sharp. And don't be late. Dinner's a busy time.'

'I'll be there on the dot,' Chloë vowed.

She luxuriated in the thought of two whole days and a night to herself, with free accommodation in this plush hotel. It would be like a mini holiday! She lingered, hoping he would point her in the direction of someone who could show her to her room.

'You'd better go back to Reception and see Linda,' Mr Ryan said impatiently, as if suddenly fed up of her presence. 'She'll find you a room in the staff quarters, and sort you out with a uniform for tomorrow.'

'Thank you, Mr Ryan,' Chloë gushed, gathering her bags together. 'It's very good of you.'

She was almost at the door when she remembered. 'Oh, yes, and could I have my bag back please?'

For a moment, a look of extreme impatience seemed to cross his face as he glanced up from some paperwork. Chloë quickly took the bag, then, before he could change his mind about the job, she left.

CHAPTER TWO

Chloë was woken by a sharp, insistent knocking on her door. For the second morning running, she was disorientated. Then she recalled that as of tonight, she was officially an employee of the Hotel Collingwood. She glanced at her alarm clock. Six o'clock. No wonder she felt so dreadful, like she'd been dragged through a hedge backwards then hit repeatedly with a mallet. It hadn't helped that she'd stayed awake for hours last night, pondering on the fact that this was the night before what was supposed to have been her wedding day, thinking about what might have been. But in spite of the earliness of the hour, the knocking showed no signs of abating. Chloë slid reluctantly out of bed, staggering blearily over to the door.

'OK, OK, I'm coming,' she muttered crossly.

As she went to open the door she caught sight of herself in the mirror. Her hair was tousled and her face still half asleep, and she was wearing her nightie. Perhaps flinging the door open wasn't such a good idea.

'Er—who is it?' she called cautiously.

'It's me, Dominic.'

The thought of a power-suited Dominic Ryan standing at the door almost made her choke on her words.

21

'What do you want at this hour?' Chloë spluttered, then remembered she was talking to her boss. 'Only,' she added quickly, 'I can't answer the door. I'm not dressed.'

'The thing is,' Dominic said, 'that someone's phoned in sick. It looks like we're going to need you this morning after all. Can you start now?'

'When would you want me down there?' she asked.

'Six thirty,' Dominic said and added gruffly, 'Thanks.'

'That's OK.'

As she moved away from the door, Chloë caught another glimpse of herself in the nightie. It was white, and for a moment she was reminded incongruously of her wedding gown, and what was meant to have been taking place today. But there was no time to think about what was happening back in Southbridge, about the chaos that was no doubt ensuring in her absence. It was already five past six, and in twenty-five minutes she had to be down in the kitchens.

She was ready with five minutes to spare, dressed in the white blouse, black skirt and frilly white apron Linda had given her the night before.

'Ah, Miss Johnson, Chloë,' her new boss greeted her on her arrival in the kitchens, where the chef was already busily at work.

At least last night's heated verbal exchanges

22

appeared to have been forgotten. Clad even at this hour in his customary dark suit, he glanced at his expensive wristwatch.

'You made it on time.'

'Of course. Mr Ryan,' she answered. 'I always keep my promises.'

For a moment their eyes locked, and Chloë was aware of some indefinable spark passing between them. Then she smiled. She was beginning to enjoy playing this new role she had created for herself. At that moment the kitchen door swung open.

'Tanya, Darren,' Mr Ryan greeted the two newcomers. 'Chloë will be joining us from today. Chloë, this is Tanya Taylor and Darren Andrews, two of your fellow waiting staff.'

'Pleased to meet you,' Chloë greeted the two.

Darren was an amiable-looking young man, with a round, boyish face and short fair hair. He stepped forward to shake her hand. Tanya, on the other hand, petite and curvaceous, with stunning red hair swept up into a pony-tail and well made-up, pretty hazel eyes, gazed at Chloë in barely concealed hostility. Chloë sensed that Tanya regarded her as some kind of rival. It was a sensation which was entirely new to her.

'Perhaps you two can show Chloë the ropes.' Mr Ryan suggested, 'as it's her first day.'

'Whatever you say. Dominic,' Tanya simpered.

Chloë had the instant feeling that these two were more than employer and employee but Tanya's smile died the moment Dominic left the kitchen, the swing doors banging noisily shut behind him.

'Dominic didn't say anything about any new staff,' she commented sulkily to Darren, ignoring Chloë.

'No,' Darren admitted, 'but Pat did phone in sick this morning. And we're delighted to have you here,' he said to Chloë.

'Thank you.' Chloë replied. 'It's—er—nice to be here!'

Tanya glowered in the background. From her evident annoyance at Darren's interest in her, it seemed as though she regarded him, too, as her property. If it had been down to Tanya, Chloë would have been left to get on with it with no assistance whatsoever. But fortunately Darren went out of his way to help her, as she learned how to take the breakfast orders, place them with the chef, and carry the food and drinks to the relevant tables.

'Don't let Dominic put you off,' a friendly voice behind Chloë said as she was about to re-enter the kitchen, aware of the watchful, brooding presence in the corner of the restaurant.

Glancing over her shoulder she saw Darren close behind her, balancing a tray full of dirty crockery.

'I'm trying not to,' she said as they entered

the kitchen. 'It's not easy.'

'I know,' Darren sympathised, as they both off-loaded their dirty dishes on the counter. 'I was the same when I first started here. Our Mr Ryan believes in personally overseeing every aspect of the running of the hotel.'

For the three solid hours of that hectic breakfast session, Chloë forgot her worries about Anthony and what today should have been. But eventually the last guests left the restaurant, and the imposing presence of Dominic Ryan strode into the kitchen where the three of them were tidying up the serving area. Once again Chloë felt her heart lurch at the sight of him. She expected him to speak to Tanya, and was surprised when he turned his attentions to her.

'Well done, Chloë. You performed well considering it was your first day. Perhaps you were right to publicise your relevant skills.'

Chloë was aware of Tanya staring at her with a mixture of hostility and curiosity. She decided to play the scene for everything it was worth.

'Thank you,' she said and with a smile she added, 'I take it that means you won't be prosecuting me under the Trade Descriptions Act?'

'I don't think you need have any worries on that score, Chloë,' Dominic replied as their eyes met again, traces of amusement twitching at the hard line of his mouth.

'I'm glad to hear it,' she said, still aware of Tanya staring at them.

'In fact,' Dominic went on, 'why don't you take the rest of the morning off? I think you've earned it.'

'Oh, thanks very much.'

Despite his hard exterior, something told her Dominic had sensed the tiredness that lurked beneath her bright manner. In spite of herself, she felt a spark of liking for him.

'Report back for duty at three o'clock sharp this afternoon,' he went on, reverting to brisker mode, before turning to leave.

'Well, someone seems to have made an instant hit with the boss,' Darren commented in mock-surprise as Chloë removed her apron. 'I should make the most of it while it lasts.'

'I intend to. I'll see you later.'

Her last view as the kitchen doors swung shut behind her was of Tanya staring after her, a thunderous expression marring her pretty face.

Chloë sat and gazed at her reflection in the mirror up in her room. It was true she looked different, the blonde hair swept boldly back from her face, green eyes and slanting cheekbones highlighted by more make-up than she would normally wear, but underneath, she was the same person who had fled Anthony and her old life only the day before yesterday.

Chloë busied herself, removing the make-up with cotton-wool and cleanser. When she had

26

finished she felt more than just superficially cleansed, she felt somehow purged. But there was still one more thing. Lifting her hands to her head, Chloë carefully removed the short, blonde wig, easing it off so that her silky, dark hair, carefully tucked up inside, came tumbling down around her shoulders.

Minutes later she slipped quietly out of the back entrance of the hotel, dressed in her old trousers and T-shirt, hair tucked under the baseball cap on her head. It was a sunny, June day with a refreshing breeze blowing off the sea, and Chloë headed east along the seafront, up the gradually ascending road until she emerged on to the cliffs that towered above the bay, following the path regularly trod by walkers.

Once she felt she was safely out of sight of the hotel, she removed the baseball cap, letting the wind whip through her hair. And then, as she strode along, it all gradually flooded her mind, her conversation with Sue, the reason why she had finally run away.

'I'm sorry to have to be the one to tell you this,' Sue had begun, genuine regret in her eyes, 'but the thing is, I was chatting on the phone to my friend, Paula, yesterday and I was explaining I couldn't see her on Saturday because of the wedding, and, well, it turns out she used to work with Anthony. She told me some things about him that I think you should know.'

Sure that Anthony was incapable of doing anything of which she would disapprove, Chloë was barely able to contain her impatience.

'There's no easy way of saying this, so I might as well get to the point.' Sue sighed. 'Apparently, Anthony is an addicted gambler, and has several, long-standing debts.'

'No!'

Chloë had gasped, interrupting her friend. It couldn't be true. That just didn't sound like Anthony at all. But then, one or two pieces began to fall horribly into place. The many times they spent apart—Anthony was probably out at the casino or the bookmaker's or wherever he went. They had decided to buy a house together, for after they were married, but Anthony had insisted on the mortgage being in Chloë's name. At the time she had banished her silly qualms to the back of her mind. Now, however, it all made horrible sense. With long-standing debts, there was no way Anthony would have been able to get a mortgage himself.

'According to Paula, Anthony lost his job at the bank because they found out about the gambling,' Sue went on.

Anthony had told her he was between jobs, that he was holding out for the right one, but now Chloë saw that no company in their right mind would employ someone with massive debts. What was worse, Anthony had obviously been intending to use her, her salary, savings, to pay off his debts.

She was surprised to discover that her overriding emotion was one of humiliation. She felt as if she had been made a thorough fool of by Anthony. He had deliberately preyed on her. She had believed Anthony to be very nearly perfect, but now she saw that was far from the truth.

Two days ago she had been convinced she loved Anthony. Now she wasn't sure what she felt for him, if anything.

Chloë glanced at her watch. Twenty-five past eleven. With a shock she recalled that she would have been getting ready for her big day now, assisted by Anthony's sisters and mother. She could see them all crowding round her, just as they had at the dress fittings, staring and criticising.

It would have been different, of course, if she'd had her own family, but her parents had been killed in a car crash when she was only a few months old. Now, at the age of twenty-three, there was no other family she was close to. Her grandparents had passed on, her father's brother lived in Australia and her mother had been an only child. Of course, there were her friends Sue, Jenny and Alison. But, wonderful though her friends were, it wasn't the same.

She wondered now what was happening back in Southbridge. Was all hell breaking

29

loose? The thought made her shiver and, involuntarily, she quickened her pace. By the time she came back to the present, she realised that she had been walking for some distance. A cafeteria loomed ahead. Its carpark was empty, and her heart rose at the prospect of a quiet seat and a refreshing drink.

As she drew closer she saw that the windswept café—Inspiration Point Cafeteria, as it proclaimed itself—looked as though it had changed little in thirty-odd years.

'Hello, can I help you?'

'Yes, a pot of tea for one, please.'

Too late, Chloë recognised the woman behind the counter. It was the woman on the train yesterday, Mary Field. She would be recognised, as she didn't have her wig on. She would just have to stay calm and hope the woman wasn't particularly observant.

'I knew I'd seen you somewhere before!' Mary said as she brought Chloë her pot of tea. 'You're that girl from the train yesterday!'

'That's right.'

Conceding defeat, she took off the baseball cap.

'I thought I recognised you.'

She placed her tea on her tray and moved along the counter hoping to curtail the conversation, but Mary moved to wait for her at the till.

'You should have told me you lived in Eccelesdon,' Mary went on. 'I assumed you

30

lived in Wareham. It's on the house,' she added as Chloë offered her money.

'Oh, no, I couldn't possibly.'

'No, I insist,' Mary argued. 'Chloë, wasn't it?'

'That's right.'

Chloë allowed herself a smile for the first time.

'Thanks very much, Mary.'

'Forget it.'

Chloë, selecting a secluded table by the window, was about to head towards it when Mary added, 'I would have waited for you yesterday if I'd known you lived in Ecclesdon.'

'I expect we were both in a rush, and I had things to do in Wareham.'

'Ah,' Mary nodded, obviously still curious.

She went to move away when Chloë said on impulse, 'Why don't you join me? If you're not busy, that is.'

'Thanks, I'd like to. As you can see we're not exactly turning them away.'

She gestured round the cafeteria, empty except for an elderly, male dog walker nursing a cup of tea, and a couple of hikers.

'What a gorgeous view,' Chloë said as they sat down.

They could see right across the bay, from the plush hotels to the west, past the gaudily-coloured amusements in the town centre, to the old wooden fishing pier stretching out in the east.

'Yes, I always say this place is aptly named. Whenever the kids are screaming, or Rob's feeling stressed out, or the books won't balance, I just look out the window. That view alone is enough to make it all worth while.'

There was a brief pause, during which they both sipped their tea.

'Funny,' Mary said, 'I've never seen you before, and then suddenly I see you twice in as many days.'

'Oh, well,' Chloë shrugged nervously. 'That's life for you.'

'So, have you got family round here, Chloë?'

'No.'

The question hit home, and for once the truth came tumbling out.

'I'm an orphan.'

'Oh, I am sorry.'

The regret was genuine in Mary's kind, maternal face. Suddenly Mary's eyes were drawn towards the door.

'Oh, excuse me a moment please, Chloë.'

'Of course.'

Chloë glanced over her shoulder as Mary moved back behind the counter. As she did so, her gaze was arrested, for the customer who had just walked in was none other than Dominic Ryan, looking devastatingly attractive in faded jeans, a striking contrast to his normal smart-suited appearance. His brown hair was windswept in a way that suited his rugged face. What on earth was he doing here?

Chloë glanced down at her tea-cup as the blush rose hotly in her cheeks. She wasn't wearing her disguise, she told herself firmly. He'd never recognise her. But her eyes were drawn back, and, to his dismay, he was staring at her. If she hadn't known better, she could have sworn a trace of recognition passed between them. It was as if he was trying to place her, but couldn't. Suddenly it was too much for Chloë and, grabbing her baseball cap, she fled.

That evening, Chloë wrote to her friend, Sue.

Sorry I've been so long contacting you, Sue, but my feet have hardly touched the ground in the last few days. How are things in Southbridge? What did Eileen say about me being away from the library for a while? More to the point, were Anthony and his family furious that I didn't turn up for the wedding? I'd better give you my address, so you can write and let me know. It's Hotel Collingwood, 51 Bayview Road, Ecclesdon.

Yes, I've found myself a job in a hotel, as a waitress. I know, it's a bit of a change from a library assistant, but I'm coping. In fact, you'd be proud of the way I've adapted to my new lifestyle. I haven't got any long-term plans at the moment. I'm just living from day to day. Please write soon, Sue, and give Jen and Ally my love, but whatever you do, don't tell Anthony that you know where I am.

Finishing the letter, she scanned through what she had written, and then signed it simply *Chloë*.

She just had time to post the letter at a box in a nearby street and get back for that evening shift. She knew she should have written to Anthony, too, as soon as she had fled Southbridge, but there was no way she was going to risk writing to him from here. He would probably take one glance at the postmark and be on his way down. Anthony was the sort of man who didn't like to take no for an answer.

That night, the last lingering guests were at one of Chloë's tables, and so she had to wait on while they sat and chatted over after-dinner coffees and liqueurs until gone half eleven.

'Why don't you get off now, Chloë?' Darren offered in the kitchen. 'I can take over here. That lot might be here till past midnight.'

'Thanks, Darren.' Chloë smiled back. 'But I'll be fine. I live here, after all, and you've still got to get home.'

'Well, if you're sure?' Darren asked doubtfully.

'Sure,' Chloë assured him. 'Push off home, before I change my mind!'

At last the party dispersed, leaving a hefty

34

tip. Chloë, her feet and back aching, quickly cleared the table and turned off the restaurant lights. The place seemed deserted. There wasn't even any sign of Dominic, which was unusual. He seemed such a workaholic that he was usually around.

As she walked through the bar to get to her room, however, she found her answer. He and another man were sitting on bar stools, lingering over a bottle of champagne. Her eyes met Dominic's. For a moment Chloë's heart pounded wildly, sure that he had finally recognised her from the café and was about to demand what she was playing at.

'Chloë,' Dominic greeted her, 'why don't you join us for a drink?'

Taken aback, Chloë answered, 'Thanks, Mr Ryan, but I think I'd better get an early night.'

'Call it staff development then. Do you like champagne?'

Calming her pang of trepidation, she walked across to the two men.

'Of course, Mr Ryan. Why?'

'You're not on duty now, Chloë. Call me Dominic, please.'

'All right then.'

'That's better. Now, pull up a seat.'

He placed a bar stool between him and his friend, which Chloë tentatively sat on, the butterflies in her stomach at odds with her confident exterior.

'This is my business acquaintance, Mario

35

Maldini. He runs the Majestic. Mario, this is Chloë, my new waitress.'

'Delighted to meet you.'

'Likewise,' she replied.

Dominic poured her a flute of frothing champagne.

'What were you celebrating?' she inquired.

Dominic shrugged.

'Being the two most successful entrepreneurs in Ecclesdon.'

Really, Chloë wondered, did the man's conceit know no bounds!

'Sorry to break up the party,' Mario said, 'but I think I've done enough celebrating for one night. My wife will be wondering where I am.'

'Shall I call you a taxi?' Dominic asked.

'No thanks, Dom.' Mario grinned. 'I think I can stagger two hundred yards down the road.'

'I'd better be going, too. I've got an early start in the morning.'

Chloë drained her glass, as Mario left.

'Don't go yet, Chloë.'

Dominic's hand on hers restrained her as she moved to get up. His touch seared through her nerves.

'Stay, tell me a bit about yourself.'

Somewhere in the back of Chloë's mind, she knew she should have been wary. There was a light of curiosity in Dominic's dark eyes.

'Have you lived in Ecclesdon long?' he probed.

'A while,' Chloë answered evasively.

'So, how come you were so desperate for a job that first night you came here? What was it you said, that you'd be sleeping on the beach if I didn't give you a bed for the night?'

'Yes, well,' Chloë mumbled, 'I was down on my luck.'

'You seem to have bounced back remarkably well.'

'Thank you. It was good of you to give me a job. You helped me out, just when I needed it most.'

'As long as you realise that I don't make a habit of it.'

Dominic's tone was businesslike once again.

'Normally quite a ruthless businessman, are you?'

'Ruthless is a bit harsh,' Dominic amended. 'I like to think hard, but fair.'

'Right,' Chloë said, amused. 'Have you been running this place long?'

'Eleven years,' he told her. 'I built it up from nothing. I put everything I've got into this place, literally. I've sweated blood to make it a success.'

'You must have had to make a lot of sacrifices.'

'You could say that, like sleep, food, a social life.'

'Just the luxuries, then,' Chloë joked gently.

For some inexplicable reason, she longed to ask him if he had ever been married, but didn't dare.

'Anyway, how did we get on to the subject of me? I thought you were supposed to be telling me a bit about yourself. You're quite a dark horse, Chloë Johnson.'

Chloë winced at the use of the false name. Somehow it jarred. Dominic stared at her more intently than ever, and their faces suddenly seemed very close over the champagne bottle and glasses. They were so close that she was sure he would notice she wore a wig.

'And the strange thing is, I keep thinking I've seen you somewhere before,' he was saying.

Chloë dropped her eyes.

'Isn't that a bit of a cliché?'

She could feel her cheeks flaming.

'Look at me, Chloë.'

Suddenly Dominic's voice was soft and quiet.

'I really must be going now,' Chloë mumbled, scraping back her stool.

This was it, she thought. He had seen through her. But once again the hand was placed on hers, gently but firmly preventing her from going anywhere.

'I said, look at me, Chloë,' he repeated.

It was as if Chloë had no choice. She lifted her head, waiting for the words to come, but they never did. Instead he leaned forward and kissed her. It was too soon after Anthony,

Chloë told herself numbly. She should never trust another man again. Yet before she knew what she was doing, Chloë was responding to Dominic's kiss.

It was unlike anything she had ever experienced before, completely different from the chaste kisses she had shared with Anthony. But it wasn't just Dominic who was different, she realised as the kiss deepened and he pulled her closer to him. It was her. Whether it was the clothes, her new identity or just the mood, she was kissing Dominic Ryan as she had never kissed anyone before.

They were interrupted by the sound of the kitchen door slamming shut. As the two of them pulled apart like naughty children, Chloë was stunned to see Tanya standing there, her hazel eyes blazing fire.

CHAPTER THREE

'Don't let me interrupt you, Dominic,' Tanya said venomously. 'I only came back to get my handbag. But I can see you've business to finish.'

And with that, she stalked off.

'Tanya didn't have to lie on your behalf,' Chloë told Dominic quietly.

'What do you mean?'

'That story about the handbag. It was obviously just a flimsy pretext to come back when she thought everyone else had gone.'

'But why would she want to do that?'

The relaxed atmosphere of a few moments earlier had gone.

'Oh, don't play dumb, Dominic,' Chloë said with a mirthless laugh. 'It was clear she hoped she would catch you alone.'

'What would Tanya want with me? What are you getting at, Chloë?' he said sharply. 'If you've got something to say, just come out with it.'

But she wasn't going to come right out and accuse him of having a relationship with Tanya. She wasn't that naïve.

'Let's just say, perhaps Tanya expected to find you in a more amenable mood than earlier this evening.'

Chloë's blasé tone hid her deep inner hurt.

The taste of his kiss was still on her lips, after all.

'Perhaps,' she added, 'perhaps it was some kind of rendezvous.'

Dominic Ryan got to his feet, with a suddenness that startled her.

'I hope you're not implying what I think you are,' he said, his voice suddenly low and serious. 'I know you're partial to the odd game of verbal ping-gong, but I'll warn you not to take things too far. I'm the boss here, remember, and I'd hate to have to fire such a valuable member of my staff.'

'Surely even you wouldn't fire someone for speaking the truth,' Chloë replied stubbornly.

'Chloë.' Dominic said slowly and patiently, as if to a stupid child, 'it's not the truth. It's a complete fabrication on your part. Tanya and I are nothing to each other. We never have been, and, if I have anything to do with it, we never will be.'

For a moment relief flooded over her. Then cynicism crept back in.

'Tanya seems to think differently.'

'That's up to her.'

'It must be a pain, being constantly followed round by a love-sick waitress,' Chloë commented, still not really believing his words. 'Why do you keep her on?'

'Tanya is a good waitress,' Dominic said firmly. 'The customers like her.'

'Like the look of her,' Chloë muttered

41

under her breath. 'Anyway,' she went on swiftly, 'I really must be going now. Like Tanya, I need my beauty sleep. Oh, and by the way, thanks for the champagne.'

Dominic Ryan stood and stared at her. Chloë Johnson certainly was an enigmatic lady. He tried for the umpteenth time to think where he had seen her before, then gave up. Wearily he moved behind the bar and began clearing away the empty champagne bottle and glasses. He sighed. Things had been going so well until Tanya had interrupted them.

He caught himself just in time. What did he mean, things had been going so well? He didn't even know what he'd been doing, asking her to have a drink with him in the first place. And besides, as he'd remarked to Joe only the other evening, she wasn't his type, with that bright blonde hair and those smart, sassy clothes. Even in his younger days, he'd preferred his women to look a bit more sophisticated.

A cold, reasoning voice interrupted his reveries. What had he been playing at, kissing one of his employees, one who wasn't even his type? Maybe it was something to do with those limpid green eyes. No, Dominic concluded as he switched out the lights and moved towards the stairs that led to his rooms, his only excuse was that Chloë Johnson was intriguing. He'd just have to watch himself, and her, more carefully in future.

Next day, it was a perfect summer's day, and Chloë had packed her costume in her shoulder bag in case she fancied a swim later. But, as she trod the soft, springy grass of the headland, she knew where her feet were leading her, to the only truly friendly face she knew round here, Mary. Of course, there was always the danger that Dominic would be at the cafeteria again, but she felt that was a risk she had to take.

At the thought of Dominic, her heart plummeted. They had virtually ignored each other at breakfast this morning. How could she have been so stupid, to get involved with another man so soon after Anthony? And not just any other man—her boss! But perhaps the most stupid thing of all was that, in spite of her better judgement, in spite of everything, she feared she might be falling for Dominic.

'Chloë!' Mary recognised her straight away, despite the baseball cap.

'Er, hi, Mary.'

Chloë glanced furtively around her but there was no-one she recognised.

'What can I get you? Tea? Or something cooler?'

'Tea, please. I always find it refreshing in the hot weather.'

Mary smiled back and suddenly, Chloë longed to confide in her, to tell her everything. But she knew that was impossible. Chloë glanced over her shoulder again. Dominic

43

could walk in at any minute.

'I think I might join you, if that's all right,' Mary said, to Chloë's pleasure. 'You'll have to excuse me jumping up if someone comes to the counter.'

'That's fine,' Chloë replied, as long as the someone wasn't Dominic!

'Where are the kids today?' Chloë asked, as she poured the tea.

'Out playing with their friends. I told them to stay within sight of the café. Anyway, I've been dying to ask you. Why did you run off like that last time?'

'Oh, yes, sorry about that.'

Chloë had her answer ready.

'You see,' she began, 'I work at the Hotel Collingwood, and the man who walked into the café the other day is my boss. And, well, you know how it is. The last thing I wanted on my morning off was to see my boss.'

'Oh, Dominic? He's fine, once you get to know him!' Mary broke in.

'You know Dominic Ryan?'

'Oh, yes.' Mary smiled. 'He popped in that day to discuss my son, Alex's, birthday present. He's his godfather, you see.'

'You won't tell him you know me, will you, Mary?' Chloë asked quickly.

She could just envisage the scenario.

'Chloë?' Dominic would ask. 'That's right, she does work for me. Green eyes, short blonde hair, smartly dressed.'

'Why not, Chloë?'

Mary was definitely curious now.

'Oh, I don't know,' Chloë gabbled, blushing. 'It's just that I like to keep my work and private life separate.'

'OK, Chloë, whatever you want.'

If Mary was suspicious, she chose to keep it to herself.

'Anyway, as I was saying, Dominic's actually quite a nice bloke.'

'You could have fooled me,' Chloë muttered.

'All right, so he can seem a bit hard and ruthless at first, but that's only his business side. I'm sure he'll grow on you. Give him a break. Goodness knows, it must have been hard enough for him, building that place up virtually from scratch.'

'Have you known him long?'

In spite of herself, Chloë was intrigued.

'Years. He and Rob, my husband, were at school together. He's had to sacrifice everything to make a success of the Collingwood.' Mary paused. 'Including his marriage.'

Chloë tried not to show her shock.

'I didn't know he'd been married.'

'Yes. I suppose the trouble was that he and Julie were too similar. Both hard-headed business people. She already had her business, a recruitment agency, when they met, and he had his. The trouble was that they never saw

45

anything of each other.'

'I see,' Chloë said drily.

She was getting a better idea of Dominic's character all the time.

'And he would have preferred the little wife who stayed at home and had his dinner on the table by six o'clock every night?'

'Something like that, I suppose,' Mary said. 'Clichéd though it sounds.'

At that moment a gang of dishevelled-looking children came rushing into the cafeteria.

'Can we have an ice-cream?'

Mary sighed indulgently.

'That's the second today. You lot'll eat me out of house and home.'

Chloë could believe it. Privately she thought Mary was too kind for her own good. Still, Mary seemed happy enough. If only she could be as contented and settled as her one day, Chloë thought wistfully.

*   *   *

'Hey, Chloë, have you got a moment?'

Chloë, on her way to work that evening, turned to the receptionist. Linda had seemed haughty, almost hostile that first night, but as Chloë got to know her better she had become quite friendly.

'It's just that I'm checking numbers for the staff beach barbecue next week and I

46

wondered if you were going.'

'Oh, I don't know.'

Chloë had heard the other staff discussing the barbecue over the past week or so, as if it was the highlight of their working year. But somehow the thought of spending an evening in the company of Dominic, not to mention Tanya, was less than appealing.

'Go on,' Linda urged. 'You'll have a whale of a time, I promise you.'

Before Chloë could protest Linda had placed a tick against her name.

'Oh, I almost forgot. There's a letter for you.'

'Oh! Thanks, Linda.'

Taking the envelope, Chloë saw that it had a Southbridge postmark and was addressed in Sue's neat, professional handwriting. She was dashing up the staff staircase when she bumped into Dominic.

'Sorry, Dominic,' Chloë muttered, blushing.

The physical contact reminded her all too painfully of the other night's kiss. Dominic showed no such discomposure.

'Chloë, I was hoping I'd bump into you. Not literally, I must admit.'

'Yes, well, sorry,' she said again. 'I know I'm late for work, but I had to put something in my room first.'

Dominic's eyes fell on the letter she was clutching.

'Love letter from the boyfriend?' he asked,

eyebrows raised ironically. 'No, you don't have to answer that. None of my business.'

Chloë felt a pang. What did he mean, none of his business? He'd made her his business the other night, when he'd kissed her. Did he think he could now discard her, like an old shoe?

'I haven't got a boyfriend,' she heard herself saying, 'at the moment. Although you're right,' she quickly went on, 'my private life is none of your business. Excuse me, please. I'm late as it is.'

He touched her arm, arresting her progress.

'Chloë, we have to talk.'

'Why? I don't see that we have anything to talk about.'

'The other night, for starters,' he said firmly. 'I don't like to leave business unfinished like that.'

'I see,' Chloë replied. 'So Tanya was right. I was just another piece of business, to be dealt with and disposed of at your convenience.'

'Of course not, Chloë,' Dominic said. 'There's no need to twist things like that. We have to get things sorted out. Unfortunately, I'm busy tonight, but we must talk some other time, as soon as possible.'

'Off out, are you?' Chloë asked with quiet sarcasm.

It was probably a date. Maybe things had thawed between him and his ex-wife. Dominic must have caught the insinuation in her tone.

'It's business, actually.'

Now it was Chloë's turn to be relieved.

'Well, have a nice time.'

She made another attempt to get past him.

'I doubt it,' he said grimly, letting her pass.
'I never mix business with pleasure. But I am
going to have things out with you, Chloë,' he
warned as a parting shot. 'Soon.'

Dominic's words were still ringing in her
ears when Chloë returned to her room after
work that night. She felt exhausted but, before
she ran her bath, she snatched up Sue's letter
which she had thrown down on the bed earlier.
Quickly she scanned its contents, her eyes alert
for a mention of Anthony's name. Sue got the
preliminaries out of the way first.

*Jenny and Alison send their love. When I
told Eileen you were going to be away
from the library for a while she said that if
it was going to be a prolonged absence
they would have no choice but to treat it
as a resignation.*

In a way Chloë was relieved at this news.
She was starting to settle in at the Hotel
Collingwood. She missed Sue and the other
girls, their weekly aerobics and their customary
Thursday night drink at the Swan. But it was
best that she put everything into her new life
now.

That was the bad news, now for the even worse news, Chloë.

Reading on with a growing sense of panic, Chloë was not surprised to learn of Anthony's anger when he found out that Chloë had jilted him. He had been in contact with Sue, and was trying to get her to tell him where Chloë was hiding. Chloë was knocked for six, but forced herself to read on.

And I'm not sure how much longer I can fob him off,

Sue went on.

Sooner or later, Chloë, I'm going to have to tell him.

CHAPTER FOUR

Hurrying past Reception on her way to the restaurant, Chloë was surprised to see Dominic behind the desk with a man and woman, both of whom must have been in their sixties. He called out to her as she passed.

'Chloë, can I have a quick word when you're finished this morning? In my office?'

Chloë was reluctant to enter Dominic's office on a one-to-one basis. But she didn't see how she could refuse in front of his two companions.

'OK,' she replied.

'Fine. See you later.'

Dominic turned back to the couple, and Chloë heard a murmur of laughter as she walked off.

The days had flown by and now the day of the beach barbecue had arrived. She was thankful that Darren wasn't on duty that morning, and that Tanya's company was shared by Pat, a friendly, maternal woman in her late thirties. A couple of days before, Darren had asked Chloë to go to the barbecue with him, and she had agreed. But she had wondered ever since whether she had made the right decision. She had no intention of becoming romantically involved with him, so was she leading him on by accepting?

Chloë knocked on Dominic's door four hours later, feeling as if she was about to enter the lion's den.

'Come in,' his voice barked.

She stepped forward into a surprisingly spacious, airy room. In contrast to the cream and burgundy opulence of the rest of the hotel, Dominic's office was businesslike and neutral, with plain white walls and beige carpet, as if even here he was keeping himself closely guarded, giving little of himself away.

'Have a seat.'

Dominic's large desk dominated the room, behind which a large window gave a spectacular, panoramic view of the sweeping coastline and rugged hills rising to the west.

'I won't beat around the bush.'

With trepidation Chloë watched as he took the phone off the hook.

'I wanted to ask if you were still coming to the barbecue tonight.'

'Well, I was intending to.'

Chloë struggled to keep her outer façade neutral.

'I'm glad to hear it.'

'You are?' Chloë asked suspiciously.

'Well, yes, of course.' Dominic sounded genuine enough. 'You see, I was hoping we could put things behind us. Make a fresh start, as it were.'

It was strange, Chloë mused, to see the normally composed Dominic Ryan looking awkward, but then he obviously found the whole business particularly embarrassing.

'Yes, I think I do see,' Chloë said coolly. 'You want to forget anything ever happened between us.'

She felt a pang of hurt that he could brush their budding relationship aside so easily. Dominic was frowning now.

'I thought that was what you wanted. The other night on the stairs, you said we had nothing left to talk about.'

'All right,' she admitted reluctantly, 'so I did say that. But only because I was scared.'

'Scared?' Dominic queried, his frown deepening.

'Yes.'

Chloë paused, wondering if she should continue.

'Scared of where it might all lead, scared of the way my feelings were running away with me.'

'And why were you so afraid of the way you felt? Because you thought I was the wrong sort of man to get involved with?'

'Yes.'

It was a little white lie, as she was loathe to get involved with any sort of man at the moment.

There was hurt in Dominic's dark eyes, but she repeated the word, wanting to hurt him as he had unwittingly hurt her.

'Yes, especially if you're the sort of man who

could use me as an excuse to duck out of another relationship before it could start to get too serious.'

Somewhere deep within Chloë a voice told her she was being unreasonable, but she ignored it.

'Not to mention,' she surged on, 'the sort of man who would employ old-age pensioners just because he could get away with paying them less.'

The hurt in Dominic's eyes was chased away by a different expression, one of bafflement.

'What on earth are you going on about now?'

'Those two people I saw you with this morning.'

Chloë voiced the assumption she'd made about their presence.

'I assumed you'd hired them to look after the hotel tonight while you're enjoying yourself at the barbecue.'

Dominic's brow magically cleared.

'Yes, that is what Margaret and Peter were talking to me about this morning.'

Chloë wondered if she saw the ghost of a smile playing around his mouth.

'Actually,' he went on, 'those two would be happy to work tonight for nothing.'

'For nothing?'

Chloë had always known this man was ruthless, but that just about took the proverbial biscuit!

'Two pensioners? How could you exploit them like that?'

To her chagrin, Dominic actually laughed.

'It's hardly exploitation. They only have to hold the fort. The guests are all invited to the barbecue.' He paused. 'As I said, they'd happily do it for nothing.' He smirked. 'Even the elderly have minds of their own, Chloë.'

'Yes, well, I suppose that's their problem, if they want to be exploited by you. You certainly had them eating out of your hand this morning.'

'What do you mean, Chloë?'

She had the definite feeling Dominic was laughing at her now.

'I mean, they seemed to like you,' she said grudgingly. 'They obviously couldn't see they were being exploited.'

Dominic's dark eyes regarded her steadily.

'Well, I hope they would like their own son.'

'Their son? What's he got to do with it?' she exclaimed, then she realised she'd been unbelievably stupid. 'Those people were your parents!'

'Got it in one!'

Chloë had no doubt he was laughing at her now.

'That's it, amuse yourself at my expense. After all, I'm only some dumb blonde waitress. Well, that's what you think, isn't it?'

'Of course not, Chloë,' Dominic replied. 'I happen to think you're a very intelligent young woman. Anyway, I apologise,' Dominic went on. 'I should have told you Margaret and Peter were my parents. Introduced you, even.'

Chloë sat up straighter in her chair, surprised.

'Do they look after the hotel every year for you, when you hold the barbecue?'

'Yes,' Dominic replied. 'I know I could get people from an agency, but they always seem quite happy to do it. Enjoy it, even. And besides it's the only way I can persuade them to take any money off me.'

'So you do pay them.'

'Of course I do.'

Chloë was doubly surprised. She had imagined Mr Ryan, senior, to be at least as enterprising a businessman as his son. But from the way Dominic was speaking, it was almost as if his parents were in need of the money.

'Why won't they accept a handout then? Too proud?'

He nodded slowly, thoughtfully nursing his coffee cup.

'Something like that. But I know what you're thinking.'

'Like father, like son?' Chloë offered, the ghost of a smile playing around her lips.

'But that's where the similarity ends,' Dominic said firmly.

'So what does your father do for a living?'

'He's an artist,' Dominic replied.

'And is he a successful artist?'

Dominic shrugged.

'Moderately, I suppose. But you know how it is. Most artists live from hand to mouth, just about scraping enough money to get by.'

'What sort of things does he paint?' Chloë asked.

'Local scenes, landscapes in oils, the odd water colour.'

'Are they good?'

Dominic looked surprised.

'Well, yes, I suppose so.'

'Mmm.'

An idea was beginning to form itself.

'Why don't you suggest to your dad that you display some of his paintings around the hotel, with discreet price-tags?'

Dominic looked sceptical.

'I'm sure my father would have asked me himself if he wanted my assistance selling his paintings.'

'Maybe he doesn't like to ask. That Ryan pride rearing its head again?' Chloë suggested lightly.

'If that's the case, surely he'd be too proud to take up such an offer now.' Dominic said gruffly. 'After all, what's changed?'

Chloë thought for a minute.

'Why don't you make it sound like a business proposition, rather than an offer of assistance? After all, that's what is it.'

'I'll think about it. But I'm not sure my

father will approve. He can be a pig-headed old buffer at times.'

Something in his tone got to Chloë.

'You shouldn't take your parents for granted. You're very lucky to have them there, always willing to help out.'

Dominic regarded her in surprise.

'I'm sure your parents would do anything to help you, Chloë.'

Chloë didn't say anything. Suddenly choked with emotion, she was unable to speak.

'Chloë?' Dominic queried, a more pressing note entering his tone.

'My parents are dead,' Chloë blurted out. 'They were killed in a car crash when I was a baby.'

She shoved back her chair, getting blindly to her feet. She couldn't bear to stay to hear Dominic voice words of sympathy, of sorrow, of dismay, words she had heard so many times before. She was almost at the door when she felt his hand on her shoulder.

'Hang on a minute, Chloë. I can't let you leave, not like this.'

Dominic's tone was awkward, as if he was uncertain how to express his genuine compassion. Slowly, reluctantly, Chloë turned her tear-stained face towards him.

'Chloë, I don't know what to say,' he said softly. 'I suppose I just took it for granted that you had parents who were always around. I can't tell you how sorry I am.'

Chloë nodded, struck by the depth of feeling in his voice. For a moment they faced each other in silence. Chloë was aware that she would have liked nothing better than to fall forward into his strong, comforting arms. Somehow she sensed that Dominic, too, was longing to pull her towards him, not with the passion of the other night, but simply to comfort her. But, maybe because of what had happened between them, he made no move towards her. Presently Chloë pulled away.

'And now, if you've finished with me, Mr Ryan—Dominic,' she said, wiping a stray tear, 'I think I'll leave. You know what they say,' she added, her hand on the brass doorknob, 'about quitting while you're ahead.'

Never mind quitting while you're ahead, Dominic mused to himself as she closed the door. More like quitting before his feelings got seriously out of control, and he surprised himself by actually caring about someone. Being friends was OK and, just now, Dominic had sensed that friends was what they were becoming. He'd never been able to discuss his father like that with anyone else.

But it was as she'd begun to reveal her past to him that he'd realised his feelings encompassed more than just friendship. He'd been stunned to learn that she was an orphan, but there was something about her, a vulnerability below the surface, that clicked into place now that he knew her background.

59

And it was this secret vulnerability that made him want to care for her, to protect her from whatever hardships the world may throw at her.

He'd begun to care for Chloë more than was good for him, and as for thinking she wasn't his type, well, suddenly short, sassy blonde hairstyles and even shorter skirts were starting to pre-occupy his every waking thought.

*   *   *

'You're looking very lovely tonight.'

'Oh, thank you.'

Sipping her drink, Chloë couldn't help wishing the compliment had come from Dominic, but it hadn't. It had come from Darren. The hotel chef was tending the large barbecue nearby, delicious smells mingling fragrantly on the balmy air. It had been a scorching day and the evening was still warm, the gentle noise of the sea mingling with the sound of the music drifting from the large portable stereo. A crowd of staff and hotel guests had already gathered on the beach but as far as Chloë could tell, Dominic was not yet amongst them.

'You look nice, too,' she offered in response to Darren's compliment. 'I'm surprised there isn't a glamorous woman on your arm tonight!'

Just then Chloë spotted Dominic, over by

the barbecue, chatting to Mark, the chef. For a moment she couldn't believe her eyes. Teamed with casual black trousers, Dominic was sporting a Hawaiian shirt! True, it was an expensive-looking, delicately-patterned affair in subtle shades of pale blue, jade green and lilac. It was just the incongruity of seeing the normally power-suited Dominic wearing such a casual garment that made her wonder if she'd had too much punch and was hallucinating.

Perhaps Dominic did have a casual relaxed side after all, Chloë thought, as she watched his face break into a laugh over a joke shared with the chef. At that moment, he turned, catching Chloë's surreptitious gaze. Their eyes locked across the crowded beach and Chloë's heart skipped a beat.

'I see the boss has arrived,' Darren said.

'What? Oh, yes. What does he think he looks like in that Hawaiian shirt?'

She attempted to cover her discomfort.

'I think it looks quite cool.'

'I suppose it is a nice shirt,' Chloë agreed reluctantly. 'It's just what's in it that leaves something to be desired!'

'Crikey!' Darren grinned. 'What's the boss done, dock your pay or something?'

'No, nothing like that,' Chloë said hastily, taking another sip of her drink.

If only it was as simple as that. Her feelings for Dominic were a tangled mixture of

61

emotions.

'Are you sure things are OK with you and the boss?' Darren asked, grey-blue eyes narrowed in sudden suspicion. 'He hasn't done something to upset you, has he?'

'No, of course not,' Chloë said breezily.

'That's all right then. But if I find out he has upset you—'

His words tailed off, and Chloë wondered what a mere waiter could actually do to his power-crazed boss.

'Thanks, Darren, you're a pal.'

Chloë smiled. It was true—Darren was nice, too nice. Why couldn't she fall in love with him, instead of complicated, unpredictable Dominic?

'Come on, let's dance.'

Darren dragged her over to the patch of sand near the stereo where people were already swaying to the rhythmic Spanish guitar music. They danced for three tracks, after which Chloë was exhausted. She laughed breathlessly as they went to find somewhere to sit down.

'Having a good time?' a familiar voice said behind Chloë, when Darren had gone in search of more drinks.

'Oh, hello, Dominic,' Chloë said, turning round. 'Er, yes, thanks. Darren's just gone to get some more punch.'

'You and Darren seem to be getting on pretty well.'

62

'He's a nice lad, Darren.'

For some reason she felt like riling Dominic.

'I could do worse.'

'Certainly.'

Then suddenly Dominic's expression darkened. Turning, Chloë saw Tanya making a bee-line through the crowd towards them.

'I'll catch you later,' Dominic said, and he was gone, slipping away into the crowd before Tanya reached them.

'I've just seen Darren,' Tanya said to Chloë, perching on a striped deckchair beside her. 'He said to tell you they've run out of punch. They've sent him back to the hotel to get some more rum. He won't be a minute.'

'Oh, right. Thanks.'

Poor Darren. It wasn't like Tanya to be carrying messages, Chloë thought, smoothing the way between her and Darren. Unless that was her way of ensuring Chloë stayed away from Dominic. It was time to set the record straight.

'Don't get me wrong, I like Darren,' Chloë told Tanya slowly. 'But there's nothing going on between us, you know.'

Tanya made no attempt to hide her disappointment.

'It would do you good to stay away from Dominic for a while. I don't mean to be rude, but he must get pretty sick of the way you fawn over him all the time.'

That was rich, coming from Tanya!

'So, you'd rather I stayed away from Dominic,' Chloë said slowly, 'and left the way clear for you?'

'Not to put too fine a point on it,' Tanya lowered her voice again, 'yes.'

So Tanya was serious about Dominic, Chloë thought. And she'd certainly dressed to kill tonight, in a strappy dark-green dress, her long red hair blowing slightly in the sea-breeze.

'Look,' Chloë said slowly, 'you don't have to see me as some kind of rival, you know.' She paused. 'Why can't we be friends?'

It seemed an unlikely friendship, but Chloë meant what she said. There was no need for her and Tanya to be enemies. If Tanya wanted Dominic, let her go after him. Despite Chloë's own feelings for Dominic, she sensed their relationship was doomed to failure. After all, what future was there with a man with whom she was doomed to live a lie?

'I don't have to see you as a rival?' Tanya echoed with a hollow laugh. 'Why, you're never out of Dominic's sight.'

'What do you mean?' Chloë asked cautiously, wondering how much Tanya knew about her and Dominic.

'I mean, that so-called meeting you had with him this morning. I saw you go into his office. You must have been in there well over an hour.'

Chloë was incredulous.

'You hung around all morning, just to spy on me and Dominic?'

'I wasn't spying on you. I was around anyway, helping with the preparations for tonight. And I'm not the only one who noticed. It's all over the grapevine.'

So the rest of the staff were starting to gossip about her and Dominic! Well, she decided, things had gone far enough.

'Look, Tanya,' she said, her voice barely audible above the pulsing music and buzz of voices, 'I can honestly tell you that there is nothing whatsoever going on between me and Dominic.'

Well, it was the truth, wasn't it?

'And now, I'd better go and see where Darren's got to.'

As Chloë neared the drinks' table, she noted out of the corner of her eye that Dominic was now tending the barbecue himself. He was even wearing the chef's hat at a jaunty angle.

'Hey, Chloë!'

She stopped dead. Ever since receiving Sue's letter she'd been jumpy, but it was only Darren greeting her.

'Sorry, I didn't get back to you but Joe's gone off and left me in charge of the punch.'

'Never mind,' she said brightly. 'I'll have a glass of your lethal punch.'

Darren was handing her a glass when a voice said, 'Chloë, could I ask for your assistance over here for one moment?'

It was Dominic, pulling rank. Chloë exchanged glances with Darren.

'Better go,' she murmured. 'The big boss calls.'

Darren's face was concerned.

'If you're sure you're all right?'

He obviously thought Dominic was going to upset her again. Chloë hoped he was wrong.

'I'll scream if I need any assistance.'

'What was that about screaming for assistance?' Dominic asked dourly as she went over to the barbecue.

'Just a little—er—private joke.'

'A joke's all very well, but not at my expense,' Dominic growled.

Chloë sighed. It was clear—the man had obviously had his sense of humour removed at birth!

'Anyway, now I'm here, what do you want me to do?' she asked brightly.

Dominic was busy turning kebabs.

'What? Oh, there's nothing much you can do at the moment. It'll be ready to serve in a couple of minutes.'

'So why did you summon me over here then?' Chloë asked quietly. 'Just for the sheer enjoyment of pulling rank, or because your ego couldn't stand the sight of me talking to Darren?'

The punch was giving her false courage and she added in a reckless whisper, 'You don't want me, but you don't want anybody else to have me either—ow!'

Chloë flinched in pain as some smoke dust from the barbecue drifted into her eye. Instantly Dominic turned away from the barbecue.

'Chloë, what's the matter? Here, have this.'

He thrust a paper serviette at her.

'Thanks.'

Chloë passed the tissue to her smarting eye. Suddenly Darren was beside them. He turned on Dominic.

'You—you brute! You've made her cry!'

Chloë pulled the serviette away from her eye in horror.

'No, Darren, it's OK!' she said hastily. 'I just got smoke in my eye.'

Darren looked unconvinced.

'I don't believe you! I bet he made you say that! All evening you've been staring at him like a frightened rabbit. I don't know what he's done to upset you, but I intend to find out.'

'No, Darren, honestly, it's the truth,' Chloë said anxiously. 'I was just helping with the barbecue and—'

'Darren,' Dominic said curtly, cutting into the conversation, 'you've clearly got the ridiculous idea into your head that for some reason I'm picking on Chloë. Now why on earth would I single her out for my criticism? Chloë is an excellent worker. I have no fault to find with her work.'

'Well, then, why was she in your office so long this morning?' Darren asked, pink-cheeked from exertion and punch. 'I'm not deaf, I've heard the rumours. What was that for, if it wasn't to give her a dressing down?'

'Darren,' Dominic grated out, 'any differences that exist between Chloë and myself have nothing to do with work. They're personal.'

'Oh, I see.' Darren nodded. 'A clash of personalities. Well, that's just as unfair a reason for dismissal as anything else. Chloë could take her case to an industrial tribunal.'

'The only person who's likely to be taking their case to a tribunal is you, Darren. My patience is being severely tried here.'

'The kebabs!' Chloë cried.

They looked perilously close to burning, besides which, she was glad of the distraction. While Dominic busied himself with the barbecue, she turned to Darren.

'Just leave it, will you? I swear I'm OK. I'll explain to you later.'

Hopefully Darren would never hold her to this, Chloë thought as he finally nodded reluctantly and moved away.

CHAPTER FIVE

'What a palaver,' Dominic muttered, whipping off his chef's hat as they flopped down on to deck-chairs with paper-platefuls of food.

Chloë sensed he wasn't talking about serving food to fifty or so hungry staff members and hotel guests.

'You can say that again,' Chloë said, deliberately choosing to misunderstand him. 'I thought that queue of people would never end. Still, at least Mark's taken over again now.'

Mark, the chef, was barbecuing a variety of delectable sweet treats. Dominic gave Chloë a pointed glance.

'You know I mean that business with Darren.'

'Oh, that.'

Dominic's dark eyes narrowed and he lowered his voice still further.

'Just what have you told Darren about us, Chloë?'

Chloë sighed. Dominic's moods seemed to change with the wind.

'Darren knows nothing whatsoever about us,' Chloë replied firmly.

Come to think of it, where had Darren got to? Suddenly she wished she was with him instead of Dominic. She felt uneasy sitting next to him, slightly away from the rest of the increasingly lively party. It could only give her workmates even more to gossip about.

'Now, can we please change the—'

Chloë broke off, her eyes transfixed by a figure on the darkening beach. Her heart skipped a beat. She'd know that dark head, that graceful build anywhere—Anthony! Then the man in the crowd turned, laughing at some remark made by his companion, and Chloë cursed her stupidity. It wasn't Anthony at all, she realised as her breath began to come more evenly again.

'What is it, Chloë?'

Dominic's dark eyes were on her, not missing a trick.

'Oh, nothing.'

Although her heart was still pounding, she managed a smile.

'Don't try and fob me off. For a moment there, you looked like you'd seen a ghost.'

Well, she had—a ghost from her other life, a life she was trying her best to leave behind. Dominic was still watching her intently, and she knew that, this time, there was no way she could talk herself out of trouble.

'Would you excuse me for a minute?'

Abruptly Chloë stood up, depositing her half-empty plate on the sand beside her deck-chair.

'I think I'd better go and see where Darren's got to.'

And before Dominic could answer she had

slipped away into the chattering, dancing throng on the sand. But she didn't go looking for Darren. Instead, she picked her way up amongst the pebbles on to the promenade. She had only gone a few paces on terra firma when she heard running footsteps behind her. Spinning round, heart pounding, Chloë saw that it was Dominic.

'Chloë,' he called, 'wait.'

Chloë quickened her pace to a run. But she didn't get far. Seconds later she felt a hand on her shoulder, and Dominic spun her round to face him.

'Stop running, Chloë,' he commanded. 'For once in your life, just face whatever it is you're running away from.'

Chloë pulled away from his grip.

'You've got it wrong. I'm not running away from anyone—anything,' she amended hastily. 'I just needed some space, that's all.'

'All right, then,' Dominic persisted, 'if you've got nothing to hide, then tell me where you came from. All I know is that you suddenly turned up on my doorstep one night. I should have asked you for references, but Joe Chambers had this hunch you'd be a good worker. I should never have listened to him.'

Chloë sighed, sinking down an to the bench seat they were standing in front of. Dominic joined her.

'You said yourself earlier tonight that there's nothing wrong with my work,' Chloë pointed out. 'Surely that's all that need concern you.'

Dominic sighed heavily.

'That's all that need concern me on a professional basis.'

He looked Chloë straight in the eye, making her heart turn over.

'But I had the feeling we were becoming more to each other than just employer and employee.'

'OK,' Chloë challenged, 'you say you want me to open up to you, but what about you? Apart from the stuff I had to force out of you about your father, you've told me nothing about your own background.'

It was Mary, she reminded herself, who'd told her about his marriage.

'There's really not much to tell,' Dominic said evasively.

'What about your private life?' Chloë pressed.

'I suppose I've had my share of relationships,' Dominic told her reluctantly, 'although I was no Romeo.'

'I'm not talking about the occasional romance,' Chloë said. 'I'm talking about deeper, more meaningful relationships.'

'Come on, let's walk back to the hotel. I can't talk here.'

'But what about the party? Won't people notice you've gone?'

'I doubt it,' Dominic said tersely, taking her

72

firmly by the arm. 'They seemed to be too busy enjoying themselves to notice.'

'I was married once,' Dominic said suddenly as they began to walk.

'Oh, really?'

Chloë pretended she didn't know.

'Yes. Needless to say, it didn't last. Irreconcilable differences, I believe they say. I should have known it was doomed. She had her own business, you see, while what I wanted was a family life, a family.'

'You mean, while you wanted her to give up her career to look after the household, you wanted to keep your business, in addition to having a family. In other words, you wanted to have it all.'

Yet even as she spoke, Chloë knew that, given the option of having Dominic's children and sacrificing her own so-called career, she'd seize it with both hands.

'I suppose you think all women should be barefoot and pregnant in the kitchen,' she said flippantly, to mask her unease.

Dominic's expression was wry as he regarded her in the semi-darkness.

'So speaks the great career woman,' he mocked gently.

'That's it, make fun of me, just because I'm a lowly waitress.'

'Well, you have to admit, Chloë, it isn't exactly wildly ambitious, not for an assertive young woman like you.'

73

Assertive! She had never been called that before!

'Thanks, Dominic. I think there's a compliment in there somewhere.'

'Seriously though, Chloë, it's not much of a job for a young woman. Is this your first job since leaving college?'

'I didn't go to college,' she admitted.

'Why not?' Dominic sounded genuinely surprised.

'With no parents there to chivvy me along, there seemed little point.'

'And you had no other family?'

'No other close family, no. My grandparents were dead, my father's brother lives in Australia and my mother was an only child.'

'I'm sorry, Chloë.'

His hand tightened around hers as they walked and Chloë was glad of the contact.

'No wonder you don't like talking about your background.'

'So I got a job in a library,' Chloë went on quickly.

'With the ultimate goal of becoming the chief librarian?' Dominic asked, with affectionate teasing in his tone.

'No,' Chloë replied honestly. 'I had no particular ambition to become anything. I left because I was fed-up of the same routine, day in day out.'

Well, one little white lie could be forgiven her. It sounded better than 'because I was

74

running away from my gambling, cheating fiancé.'

'And why do you think you were so lacking in ambition?' Dominic asked.

'Because I lacked confidence, I suppose. Oh, I'd learned to be quietly assertive with the borrowers, and of course there were the carers at the children's home where I was brought up, but I'd never had anyone close to me to tell me I was clever, pretty or simply a worthwhile person.'

She stopped abruptly.

'Now it sounds like I'm making excuses for myself.'

'Chloë,' Dominic said firmly, pulling her to a halt, 'I've never met anyone who made less fuss about coming from an underprivileged background.'

Before Chloë knew what he was doing, Dominic had raised his hands to cup her face, as if he was studying every detail. Chloë's heart beat faster.

'By the way,' Dominic added softly, 'I think you're a clever, beautiful, worthwhile person.'

Then he lowered his head and kissed her, pulling her close. When they eventually pulled apart, Chloë was breathless. They walked on in silence, this time with Dominic's arm draped casually around her shoulders.

Then he said slowly, 'I meant what I said just now, you know, about you being clever and beautiful. I didn't just say it because I wanted to kiss you.'

'Yeah, pull the other one,' she said, but secretly, Chloë was pleased.

'You know,' Dominic went on, 'I'd never have thought of you as lacking confidence. But it explains a lot.'

'Like what?'

'The way you dress, the way you present yourself generally.'

'Oh, so it's back to this, is it?'

Chloë sighed. Just when they'd seemed to be getting along so well.

'You look fine,' Dominic assured her. 'It's just, well, it's as if you're trying too hard. You don't need all that make-up, or those slinky clothes. And what colour is your hair naturally? Dark? You've got gorgeous natural colouring, Chloë. You should have more confidence in your own natural beauty.'

Chloë was cross, and amazed. She had never known Dominic could talk at such length, nor so poetically.

'Thank you, Dominic, for the beauty tips, but I think women should be able to dress for themselves, and that means dressing however they want.'

'Even if some women dress the way they do due to a basic lack of self-confidence?'

'I don't lack confidence now,' Chloë protested. 'I've changed since the days I was telling you about.'

'Good,' Dominic said.

They were nearly back at the hotel now.

'Let's go in the back way,' he suggested. 'I don't feel up to facing my parents and their well-meaning questions.'

'Dominic?' Chloë asked as they sneaked round the back way up a side-street. 'What about your wife? How did she dress?'

'Ex-wife,' he corrected tersely. 'I don't know. She was a power-dresser, I suppose. But she certainly used her femininity if she thought it would give her an advantage in business.'

Chloë stopped walking, forcing him to answer.

'In what way?'

'What? Oh, short skirts, plenty of make-up, stiletto heels.'

It was beginning to make sense to Chloë now.

'And you prefer women to be bereft of make-up, in sack-cloth and ashes in the kitchen.'

'Barefoot and pregnant, I know,' Dominic finished wearily. 'Anyway, that's enough about my ex-wife. That's over with, finished. Can we just forget about it? As it's so early, would you like to join me for coffee?'

Chloë paused. Was it wise to enter the lion's den with Dominic?'

'Coffee sounds good,' she said slowly.

Chloë was surprised to discover that Dominic's suite was not as bland as his office. Instead it was tastefully furnished in keeping with the large Victorian house of which it was part. The effect was both cosy and refined.

'You've got a lovely apartment,' Chloë commented approvingly as they stood in the sitting-room.

'Thanks,' Dominic answered succinctly. 'Right,' he went on, 'coffee.'

Suddenly her appetite for coffee had vanished.

'Actually, perhaps I'll leave the—'

Instinctively Chloë glanced up at him. It was as if what happened next was inevitable. Dominic's mouth descended on hers, and he kissed her with startlingly passionate intensity. Chloë melted into his arms, powerless to do anything but respond to him. At first the kiss was almost fierce in its passion, as if both were giving vent to the pent-up emotion between them. Chloë turned towards him, as her hands caressed the warm nape of his neck.

'Oh, Chloë,' Dominic said, letting out a long, ragged breath. 'We shouldn't be doing this.'

Somehow the sound of his voice brought her to her senses. Chloë wriggled out of his embrace.

'Too right we shouldn't!'

Dominic frowned at her sudden change of mood.

'What's up now?'

'I must need my head testing! You virtually admitted yourself that the only relationships you could handle these days were quick flings.'

'Are you telling me that you regret that kiss?'

Chloë wished he didn't look so handsome.

'Regret it? Of course I do. I must have been mad.'

Somehow she pushed from her mind the mood of intimacy that had made it seem the most natural thing in the world to kiss him.

'I have no intention of becoming just another one of your short-lived relationships, or a Tanya, or even a Julie.'

'What on earth do you mean, Chloë?'

'I mean,' Chloë explained, 'that I have no desire to be treated like a mere item on the work agenda. Your marriage failed because of your refusal to meet your wife halfway.'

Dominic's eyes were glittering dangerously now.

'Chloë, you know very little about my marriage, other than what I told you in a moment of stupidity. Our marriage didn't just break up because I wanted to have kids and she didn't. It went deeper than that. It was a fundamental clash of personalities. The crux of the matter was, we just didn't love each other enough.'

'Is that the truth,' Chloë wondered aloud, as she moved towards the door, 'or just a convenient explanation?'

Suddenly Dominic seemed exasperated.

'Look, Chloë, how do you have the nerve to

tell me I'm treating you badly, when you don't even care enough about me to tell me about yourself? God knows I tried hard enough to coax it out of you. I just feel this relationship's a bit one-sided at the moment.'

'What relationship?' Chloë asked pointedly, and then made her escape, away from his questions and painful home truths.

* * *

'Hello, Chloë, isn't it?'

'Er, yes, that's right. And you're Mr Ryan's parents?'

Chloë stood reluctantly beside the restaurant table where Dominic's parents, Peter and Margaret, were sitting. She'd been dismayed to see them in the restaurant that evening, and even more so when she realised they were in her section. Now she flicked open her notepad and smiled a forced smile.

'Are you ready to order?'

'I think so,' Margaret replied. 'It always seems so funny, ordering something from your son's restaurant. But Dominic insisted we had dinner on the house, before we leave in the morning.'

'You must be very proud,' Chloë said abruptly but she kept her best waitress smile on her face.

'We are. It's a lovely hotel, and soon the walls are going to be adorned with wonderful paintings, aren't they, Peter?'

Peter Ryan, like his wife, looked younger than his years. Dominic had inherited his father's build, while he got his colouring from his mother.

'I'm not sure adorned is the word I'd use myself,' Peter said, his face breaking into a grudging smile. 'But, yes, Dominic has offered to display my paintings around the hotel, and I've agreed.'

'Dominic's always having these good ideas,' Margaret said, very much the proud mother. 'That's why he's such a successful businessman.'

'It's an excellent idea,' Chloë commented, feeling she should say something. 'I shall look forward to seeing your paintings, Mr Ryan. I'm sure they're very accomplished.'

'Is everything all right here?' a cool voice broke in. 'Only there are other guests waiting to be served, Chloë.'

It was Dominic, Chloë managed to note, without meeting his eye. The memory of the other night still hung heavy between them.

'Oh, nonsense, boy.' Peter's father said. 'It's early and the restaurant's half-empty. That other waitress is seeing to those people over there. I was just about to tell young Chloë here what a beautiful face she's got. Don't you agree, Dominic?'

'What? Er, oh, yes.'

Dominic seemed surprised by his father's

words, and was now studying her face, brows lowered in consternation, as if searching for the beauty the older man could see.

'Yes,' he said slowly, meeting Chloë's eyes. 'I suppose you're right.'

'It obviously takes an artist's eye to see it,' Chloë muttered, to cover her embarrassment.

'But Dominic's an artist as well,' Peter said. 'Aren't you, son?'

'What?' Chloë said in utter surprise. 'An artist? I don't believe it.'

'It's true, isn't it, son?' Peter persisted. 'Got quite a bit of natural talent.'

Dominic grunted. Now it was his turn to be embarrassed.

'Well, you don't get much time for prancing around in an smock when you've got a hotel to run,' he replied.

Chloë tried to picture Dominic in an artist's smock and beret and gave up!

'Anyway,' Dominic muttered, moving off, 'I've got things to do. Chloë, take that order and let's see you look lively. Mum, Dad, if you've decided what you're having . . .'

'Don't take any notice of him,' Margaret confided as Dominic moved off. 'He's been moody ever since he was a little boy. One minute as pleasant as anything, the next—'

She snapped her slender fingers, as if to indicate the breaking of a mood.

'It's all right,' Chloë replied, appreciating the older woman's concern. 'I'm used to it by now. You know what bosses are like.'

Margaret laid a reassuring hand on her arm, her dark eyes looking straight into Chloë's anxious green ones.

'Just remember, the things Dominic says, he doesn't always mean.'

Gazing back at Margaret, Chloë found herself wondering exactly how much she knew, or guessed, about her and Dominic.

A few days later, Chloë headed down to the beach first thing. She liked this time of day, when the beach was virtually deserted. Whenever she wasn't on duty, and the weather was fine, she came down here for an early-morning swim. It was beautiful today, with a hazy July sun and that early-morning coolness in the air.

She took off her baseball cap. A slight breeze ruffled her dark hair as she strolled down to the sand. She knew that there was a chance she might see someone she knew, but today the only thing that mattered to her was the blissful sense of freedom she felt, completely alone.

During the past few days she and Dominic had all but ignored each other. She had tried not to think about the night of the barbecue, but for some reason she had felt strangely depressed since they had argued and Dominic had accused her of keeping secrets from him. But yesterday, something had happened to lighten her mood. She had received another letter from Sue. She wrote that Anthony had a new girlfriend, and that rumour had it they were soon to be engaged. He hadn't wasted any time, Chloë thought.

Chloë had written straight back, expressing her relief. If Anthony had a new woman in his life, there seemed little chance he would come after her now. Perhaps at last she could get on with her new life.

Deep in her thoughts, it was only as she neared the sand that she noticed a ginger-haired boy of about twelve splashing out of the shallows. He was wearing swimming shorts and his face was pale and anxious.

'Help! It's my mate! I think he's drowning!'

'What?'

The colour drained from Chloë's face as she scanned the water.

'Where is he?'

The boy pointed to where, far out to sea, a small figure was just visible in a huge black inner tube. The tide was turning, and he was being swept out.

'Tom stayed the night with me. We just came down for a swim. Mum and Dad don't know.'

The boy's words tumbled out as Chloë glanced frantically around but there was no-one else in sight, only an elderly dog-walker. She'd never done life-saving before, but there was no-one else, and she knew it might be too late by the time the emergency services got there.

'Help!' she called out the elderly dog-walker. 'There's a boy in trouble. Ring the emergency services and contact the coastguard.'

As the old lady hurried off, Chloë quickly pulled off her shorts and T-shirt and ran into the shallows. As soon as the water was deep enough, she took a deep breath and dived in. By the time she reached the boy he'd lost his grip on the huge inner tube and was bobbing under. Chloë took another deep breath and dived under the water, legs kicking frantically as she tugged him to the surface, turning him on to his back. He was still conscious, just. She cradled the boy's head above the water and began to swim back to the beach, thankful for all the times she'd seen it done on television. The swim back was tougher, as they were moving against the current, and the additional weight didn't help.

When they reached the shore Chloë was exhausted, her legs like lead. To her relief the police and ambulance had arrived, as well as a small crowd of passers-by and holidaymakers. Ambulance crew and police swarmed around them, bearing away the boy and wrapping him in a blanket.

'Well done, love. You probably saved his life,' a female member of the ambulance crew said, folding a blanket round Chloë's shivering shoulders. 'Do you feel OK?'

'Fine, just cold,' Chloë replied through chattering teeth. 'And tired.'

'Can we ask you some questions, miss?' a young policeman asked.

She heard the click of a camera shutter and, whirling round, saw that she had been snapped by a passing holidaymaker. Suddenly the seriousness of the situation hit her. Here she was, undisguised, with a small crowd swarming round her. And any minute now she could be caught on film!

'If you don't mind,' she told the policeman, 'I'd like a sit down first, get my breath back.'

'Yes, yes, of course,' the young man said, backing off.

Chloë grabbed her bag and clothes, glancing round for the boy she'd rescued. He was still swathed in the blanket, hair plastered to his head, but he appeared to be coughing heartily, and some colour had returned to his face. Having seen enough, Chloë took to her heels and fled.

CHAPTER SIX

It was early the following morning when Chloë saw the headlines. She'd spent a quiet day the day before, recovering from the morning's incident at the beach and hadn't seen anyone from the hotel. Exhausted, she'd gone to bed early with a book, not even bothering to look in on the staff TV lounge to catch the early evening news as she often did.

The Hotel Collingwood provided complimentary morning papers served with breakfast, and so it was that Chloë, juggling plates and taking a breakfast order, spotted the headline **Mystery Girl Rescues MP's Drowning Son** and she found herself staring straight at a small, blurred, but unmistakable photo of herself. And it wasn't the local rag, but the front page of one of the national newspapers.

The man she was serving followed the direction of her gaze.

'Quite a story, isn't it?' he commented. 'And right on our doorstep, too.'

'Yes, it is amazing,' Chloë said, a little unsteadily.

'You don't know her, do you? There's a number here to ring if you do. The MP's offering a reward.'

'I don't think so.'

87

Thank goodness no-one seemed to have recognised her—yet.

The guest held the paper towards her.

'Here. Have a better look.'

'Thanks.'

Chloë took the newspaper, absentmindedly putting the plates down and sinking on to a vacant chair at a nearby table. Suddenly her legs didn't seem to have the strength to support her. Quickly she scanned the article. Underneath the fuzzy photo of herself was the caption, **The mystery dark-haired beauty, snapped by a member of the public before she disappeared. Do you recognise this woman? If so, ring—**

Chloë's attention drifted away from the number back to the main article. She quickly realised why the story had made the front-page news. The boy she had rescued was the son of Charlotte Burrows, a high-profile, single-mother MP for the local constituency.

'I simply don't know how to thank this woman, Ms Burrows said. Other than to say that she truly is a heroine. If she can get in contact with me, I will be able to thank her, and reward her, in person.'

The report went on to say it was a miracle the raven-haired girl, thought to be about twenty, of tall, slim build, was caught on film at all. Holidaymaker, Lawrence Daniels, managed to get a picture.

Chloë experienced a momentary pang of

sympathy for the anxious, relieved Charlotte Burrows. She was never going to be able to thank her son's rescuer in person, because there was no way Chloë was going to ring that number and reveal herself.

'Chloë!'

It was Dominic's voice, low but insistent.

'I would appreciate it if you would extract your head from that rag and start serving some guests.'

'Oh, yes, Dominic—Mr Ryan, of course,' Chloë stammered.

'It's our fault,' the guest offered. 'We said she could look at our paper.'

Dominic looked at the man, as if he had taken leave of his senses.

'Yes, sir, of course,' Dominic said with scrupulous politeness. 'But now that your waitress has enjoyed her little break, I'm sure she won't mind getting on with serving you.'

When Chloë finally clocked off she was waylaid by Linda, on reception.

'A Mary Field rang for you earlier, Chloë. I said you were on duty, and she asked you to get in contact with her as soon as possible.'

Of course, Mary knew her in her old identity and would have recognised her in the photo. Chloë's overworked heart started to pound again.

'Do you want to use the phone?' Linda was asking.

'No thanks, Linda.'

Chloë didn't even have Mary's number, but she would far rather talk to Mary in person.

'I was going round to see her anyway.'

As an extra precaution Chloë tied her dark hair back into a ponytail, before tucking it into her baseball cap. Then she pulled the brim of the cap as far forward as possible, obscuring most of her face. If she walked fast, with her head down, there was a good chance people wouldn't recognise her. As it turned out, it was an overcast day with the threat of rain, and it seemed that holidaymakers had opted for a day indoors.

A more than usually excitable Mary pounced on her the moment she set foot inside the empty café. Her friend swept up to the door, turning the sign to **Closed**.

'There's been virtually no custom anyway,' she justified herself. 'Now sit down and tell me all about it, this instant! I couldn't believe it when I saw your face on the telly, and all over the papers!'

'What about the kids?' Chloë asked, glancing anxiously around her.

'At a friend's,' Mary said. 'We've got the place entirely to ourselves.'

Letting out a long breath, Chloë pulled off her cap, and sat down.

'Well, what is there to tell?'

'What is there to tell!' Mary echoed incredulously. 'Chloë Vale, you dark horse! Now I want to know all the details, and why you ran off afterwards.'

'Well, it all happened pretty much as you read it in the papers.'

'That makes a change,' Mary commented. 'The tabloids telling an accurate story! Still, I'd like to hear it straight from the horse's mouth.'

Chloë took a deep breath.

'Well,' she began, 'it was my day off, so I went down to the beach for my usual early-morning swim.'

She recounted the story, more or less as it happened.

'And as soon as I'd dragged the boy back to dry land, the emergency services took over, and that was that,' she ended.

'Except that the boy turned out to be the son of Charlotte Burrows.'

'Exactly,' Chloë agreed succinctly.

'So,' Mary asked, eyes agog, 'have you phoned that number in the papers yet?'

'No,' Chloë said shortly. 'And I'm not going to.'

'Not going to? But, Chloë, you've got to. Even if you don't care about the financial reward, think about that poor woman. She's desperate to meet the woman who saved her son, and thank her in person. Are you going to deprive her of the opportunity of doing that?'

'I'm sorry, Mary,' Chloë said, 'but I'd really rather there was no publicity.'

'But why?' Mary sounded baffled. 'What's stopping you? Are you shy?'

'No,' Chloë replied instantly. 'No, it's not that.'

'Well, then. What is it?'

Chloë stared at Mary across the table.

'It's a long story,' she said dismissively.

'I've got all morning.'

Chloë hesitated. Could she confide in Mary what she was unable to confide in Dominic?

'You remember the first day I met you, how I let you believe I was from round here?'

'Yes.'

'Well, that wasn't true. I come from Southbridge, in Sussex. That first day I met you on the train, I was running away.'

'You know,' Mary burst out, 'that first day, I sensed you were hiding something! But what were you running away from?'

'My fiancé.'

'Your fiancé?'

How could Mary be expected to understand that Anthony wasn't like other husbands-to-be?

'I wasn't just running away from Anthony. I was running away from a wedding I didn't want to go through with, from all the lies I'd been told.'

Slowly, painfully, she explained to Mary about Anthony, his gambling, his debts, his getting the sack and, worst of all, the way he'd been using her, for her scant income, and her ability to put a roof over his head.

'What a rat!' Mary said feelingly.

To her surprise, Chloë felt quite cool and calm, realising that neither Anthony's looks, nor anything else about him, meant anything to her now.

'As soon as I found out about him,' she went on, 'I realised I didn't want to marry him. I didn't know what to do.' She shrugged. 'My parents are dead, and I haven't got any close family in this country. So I decided to run away. It's pure chance I ended up here. And, in case Anthony decided to chase after me, I changed my identity.'

'Changed your identity?' Mary echoed. 'How did you do that.'

'Simple enough. Different clothes, more make-up and, the masterstroke, a blonde wig.'

She paused, a little breathless after her confession.

'You were the last person to see me in my old identity. Everyone down here, Dominic, the other staff at the hotel, know me as a blonde.'

'Yesterday, you weren't wearing your disguise,' Mary observed.

'No,' Chloë admitted. 'I like to escape sometimes, be myself. That's why, in a way, it was a relief you knew me as Chloë Vale, dark-haired, quietly-spoken Chloë Vale.'

Mary was nodding.

'So that's why you didn't want me to tell Dominic I knew you, because the Chloë he knew, and the Chloë I knew, were two very different women.'

'That's right. And that's why I ran away that day he came in here.'

'And there was I telling you that Dominic wasn't such a bad person, when all the time you had your own good reasons for avoiding him.'

Suddenly, to her horror, Chloë started to blush. It was as if she couldn't even talk about Dominic now without turning into a gibbering idiot!

'Chloë, are you all right? Oh, no, you and Dominic aren't—'

'An item? No. But we are sort of involved with each other.'

'Good heavens,' Mary breathed, 'what a mess. Still,' she went on, 'I did have my suspicions. It was the way you talked about him. I thought you were a bit too vehement in your dislike of him. It's always a sure sign.'

'But I do dislike him,' Chloë protested, feelingly. 'It's just that, unfortunately, I think I love him, too.'

And with that she burst into tears.

'At least there's one thing I don't have to worry about,' she sniffled fifteen or so minutes later when Mary had plied her with tea, serviettes, and a shoulder to cry on.

'What's that?' Mary asked as she poured the last of the tea.

'Anthony seeing my picture in the papers and coming after me.'

94

'What makes you so confident?'

'He's got a new girlfriend,' Chloë told her. 'They're supposed to be getting engaged. Anthony won't bother traipsing down here to find me now.'

*　　*　　*

The wind and rain blew in straight off the sea, buffeting the umbrella Chloë had borrowed from Linda. The weather had finally broken, but she had fancied a walk into town. What a week it had been, Chloë reflected as she walked. First the barbecue, the night she and Dominic had argued, and then there had been that business with the drowning boy, and suddenly Chloë had found her picture in every national newspaper. In a way, it had been a relief to confess the whole, complicated story to Mary yesterday.

'Lovely weather for ducks,' the chemist assistant commented as Chloë handed over the money for her bottle of shampoo ten minutes later.

Taking the carrier bag, Chloë just smiled her thanks and moved off. She didn't know what instinct made her look back, but as she did so, she saw Anthony! Although she was aware how deceiving appearances could sometimes be, when he turned slightly, a cold hand gripped her heart as she realised that she was not mistaken. She'd know that profile anywhere. He must have been standing right behind her in the queue!

Thank goodness she hadn't spoken to the sales assistant. Miraculously, Anthony didn't seem to have noticed her, and somehow she managed to make her way out of the shop. The first thing that met her eyes was the car opposite the taxi rank. Obviously parked in a hurry, the car's hazard warning lights were flashing, and there, at the cashpoint beside it, was Dominic.

Chloë glanced over her shoulder again but there was no sign of Anthony. She quickened her pace, reaching the car at the same time as Dominic.

'Chloë!' Dominic exclaimed, surprised to see her. 'Can I offer you a lift?'

'I thought you'd never ask,' she said gratefully, and she flung open the passenger door and all but hurled herself inside.

Dominic still looked taken aback as he slid into the seat beside her, dusting a smattering of raindrops from his hair and clipping on his seatbelt.

'I nearly didn't offer you a lift,' he admitted, as the engine purred into life, but Chloë was busy watching out of the rain-spattered window as two custorners emerged from the chemist's, but neither of them was Anthony.

'Chloë?' Dominic repeated, more sharply. 'I was saying, I nearly didn't offer you a lift. I thought you'd bite my head off.'

'What? Oh, yes, well, I'm glad you did.'

Now that she was safe inside Dominic's car, she was uncertain how to behave. Suddenly her passionate relief and gratitude had vanished.

'For a minute there I thought—oh, well, never mind.'

He frowned, turning his attention to the driving.

'You thought what?'

It was as if all her pent-up fear and resentment towards Anthony had to be vented on Dominic.

'That I'd relented about the other night?'

'Relented?' Dominic echoed with an empty laugh. 'You make it sound as if you were the wronged party!'

'Whereas, from the tone of your voice, I gather that you feel it was the other way round?' Chloë asked coolly.

'Well, I'm the one being kept in the dark,' he commented as they drove back along the seafront. 'Just now I almost thought you were pleased to see me. I might have guessed you were only using me for a lift home. Of course I don't mind giving you a lift, Chloë,' Dominic said wearily as they pulled into the hotel's staff carpark.

There was a concerned, almost caring note in his voice that made her strangely uncomfortable. It was unbelievable that because of Anthony. she would have to leave

Dominic behind for ever. Anthony, she thought. What on earth was he doing here in Ecclesdon?

CHAPTER SEVEN

Of course, she could always run now, tonight, Chloë reminded herself later as she stood beneath a hot shower. But it was now dark outside, and the rain was still battering down relentlessly. No, tomorrow would be soon enough. She would write Dominic a letter of resignation, leave it at Reception, and depart before anyone was up. She hated to let them all down like that, but she didn't see that she had any other option.

Wrapped in her bathrobe, Chloë dried her silky, dark hair. Suddenly it struck her that she had no idea where she was going, or whether she would change her identity again when she got there. Was she going to be on the run from Anthony for the rest of her life? Shuddering slightly, she applied her make-up, then slipped on the silky white blouse, tucked it into the short black skirt and stepped into her black court shoes. Finally she pinned up her hair, tucking it expertly into the wig.

' 'Evening, Chloë,' Dominic greeted her as she entered the bar.

Little did he know that this was the last evening they'd ever spend together, and what should it matter to him, anyway?

'Good evening, Dominic.'

She looked away quickly. The bar was quiet.

Joe had the night off and Tanya was standing in behind the bar, being chatted up by a male customer.

'Cheers, gorgeous. By the way, have you ever thought of auditioning for Baywatch?'

Something inside Chloë froze. She'd know that voice anywhere. Somehow, she forced her legs to carry her through the bar into the restaurant. It was still empty and Chloë peered through the glass of the dividing door. It was Anthony all right, lounging on a bar stool and chatting and laughing. The sight of him left Chloë totally cold. How on earth had he found her here? Was it just an unfortunate coincidence?

'Hiya, Chloë.'

Chloë almost jumped out of her skin.

'Oh, hi, Pat.' She smiled. 'I didn't know you were here.'

'So I gathered. You look deathly pale. Are you feeling all right?'

'Yes, well, actually,' Chloë replied, 'I have got a bit of a headache, and my throat is a bit sore,' she added croakily. 'But apart from that, I'm fine,' she went on, feeling guilty at the lie.

'Don't be silly,' Pat said briskly. 'It sounds to me like you're coming down with the flu. You go off up to your room, and tuck yourself up in bed with a nice hot drink.'

'But I hate to leave you in the lurch,' Chloë protested feebly.

'We'll manage,' Pat assured her. 'I'll let

Dominic know, and he can ring up Darren.'

Pat's kind, motherly face regarded Chloë for a moment.

'You and Darren were quite an item at the party the other night. For a minute I thought you two might get it together.'

Until Chloë had disappeared followed by Dominic, Chloë wondered how much the other staff knew, or suspected, about her and Dominic. Not that any of it would matter after tomorrow.

'Anyway, you go on and get yourself to bed, and leave everything else to me. I'll explain to the boss.'

'Thanks, Pat.'

Chloë slunk stealthily back through the bar. She was about to set foot on the stairs when a voice behind her made her stop.

'Where are you going, Chloë?'

She turned to face Dominic.

'Up to my room. You see, I—'

Somehow, face to face with Dominic, she was unable to lie so plausibly.

'You what?' Dominic was demanding, tall and threatening.

Suddenly Chloë longed to tell him the truth, that she simply had to get away from Anthony, but she knew that confiding in Dominic was the one thing she couldn't do.

'I wasn't feeling well, and Pat thought I might want to go and lie down.'

'Oh, Pat did, did she? And did it occur to

101

you to mention to me that we were going to be a waitress short tonight?'

'Pat said she would tell you,' Chloë muttered.

'And you didn't have the courtesy to inform me yourself?'

Dominic was being uncompromising, even by his own standards.

'No. Sorry.'

'Anyway, you look OK to me. You seem to have plenty of colour in your cheeks, and your eyes are clear. In fact, you look pretty darned good for someone on her deathbed.'

'I never said I was on my—' Chloë started, but Dominic silenced her.

'Go on then, go off up to bed or out to meet your boyfriend or whatever it is you're planning to do once my back is turned. No, I didn't mean that,' he pulled himself up abruptly. 'If you're sick, I wouldn't expect you to work. Nor would I want you to.'

'It's all right,' Chloë heard herself saying haughtily. 'I'll work tonight.'

'No, no, Chloë.' Dominic sounded shameful. 'I didn't mean that crass remark about meeting your boyfriend. Go upstairs and get yourself to bed.'

But the remark had rankled. Dominic knew she wasn't really sick. He wasn't stupid.

'I'm going back to the restaurant. I'm fine, honestly.'

'Chloë, don't be ridiculous.'

For a minute Chloë thought he was going to push her bodily upstairs. Then he took a step back from her.

'Very well, have it your own way.'

'Thank you.'

And, head held high, Chloë swept past him. Only in the restaurant did her victory suddenly seem rather hollow. She must have been mad to have actually argued with Dominic for the privilege of working tonight! The fear returned, threatening to overwhelm her. Then she caught a glimpse of her reflection in the glass of the door. It looked nothing like the self she had known all her life. The face that stared back at her was not only glamorous but assured, confident. Maybe she would be OK. After all, what were the chances of Anthony recognising her, the way she looked now?

'Chloë!' Pat pounced on her. 'I thought I sent you upstairs to bed.'

'Yes, well, I met Dominic on the way and—'

'And he persuaded you that it was more than your job was worth to take tonight off sick. Honestly, that man's such a slave-driver.'

Suddenly Pat's expression changed to a forced smile.

'Good evening, Dominic.'

'Good evening, Pat. Hello again, Chloë. Can I have a word?'

Her heart sinking, Chloë went over.

'Yes?'

'What have you been saying to Pat?' he said

in a dangerously low voice.

'Nothing. I didn't say a word.'

'Well, perhaps you should explain to her that you chose to work tonight of your own free will.'

'Yes, Dominic.'

'And now, if you really are well enough to work, would you please get over to that gentleman and serve him?'

Dominic had been so indifferent to her since the night of the party, so cold, cruel, even. She'd hate to leave tomorrow on such bad terms with him. Oh, why did her life have to be such a huge, almighty mess? She trudged over to the diner's table.

'Hello, Chloë,' Anthony said quietly, without looking up from the menu.

Stunned, Chloë's mouth opened but no sound came out. And then he did look up, turning the full, charming effect of his dark-lashed grey eyes, and wide, easy smile on her.

'Well, aren't you even going to say hello to me, then?'

'Hello, Anthony,' Chloë said nervously.

'Quite a transformation from demure Chloë Vale. What was that name you go by now? Ah, yes, Chloë Johnson. Very imaginative, I must say.'

'What do you think you're doing here, Anthony?'

'My, my. So you've got the new temperament to match the new image. What happened, Clo? Did this place send you on an assertiveness course?'

'I got out from under your thumb, that's what happened,' Chloë said in a low voice.

'And getting out from under my thumb meant turning yourself into some kind of floozy, did it?'

'I am not a floozy,' Chloë said struggling to control her anger.

'Could've fooled me. It must have been a pretty recent transformation. When I saw your picture in the paper, you looked just like your old self.'

'Yes, well, it's a long story,' Chloë muttered.

'I almost didn't recognise you in town this afternoon,' Anthony went on. 'I was behind you in the queue in the chemist's, you know. I wouldn't have known it was you, but when you handed over the money, I saw that ring on your little finger, and something clicked, instantly.'

Chloë lifted her right hand, staring at the signet ring left to her by her mother. It had never occurred to her to remove it.

'Of course, I couldn't let on I'd seen you,' Anthony was going on, 'but I was determined not to lose sight of you. So I watched out of the shop door as you got into that bloke's car and drove off, then I jumped in a taxi and followed you and, hey presto, I knew you must be staying or working here.'

'Staying here!' Chloë hissed scornfully. 'As if

I'd be able to afford it. You know, Anthony, I never had half as much money as you thought. Perhaps if you'd realised that, you'd never have got involved with me in the first place.'

'What d'you mean?'

The restaurant was starting to fill up with diners and any minute now Chloë knew Dominic would remind her not to neglect her duties.

'Look, I can't talk now,' Chloë said sullenly. 'And to be honest, Anthony, I don't really want to talk to you, ever.'

As she turned to move away, Anthony raised his voice.

'I said, what did you mean. Chloë?'

'All right than,' she hissed furiously, 'if you really want to know, I found out that you were a cheating, deceiving, gambling rogue.'

Anthony didn't look shocked, merely nodded resignedly.

'I guessed someone had been blabbing to you, or you'd been snooping around. Otherwise, why would you have run away like that?'

'I ran away because I found out you'd been using me. I don't know why you've come here, Anthony, because I'm not coming back to you, ever.'

She turned to move away, but Anthony stood up, grabbing her wrist.

'I've come here to take you back to marry me. It's what I want, it's what my family wants.

You premised to be my bride, Chloë, remember?'

Chloë snatched her wrist away angrily.

'I made that promise in good faith, a faith that you betrayed.'

'What on earth is going on, Chloë?'

A low, angry voice behind her cut into the heated exchange. Chloë spun round, wondering how much Dominic had overheard.

'Dominic, I'm sorry—I was having a bit of a problem with this diner.'

Well, that wasn't a lie.

'Hang on a minute!' Anthony interrupted. 'You're the bloke with the flash car I saw earlier today.'

He turned to Chloë.

'So who is he, Chloë?' he smirked. 'Your sugar daddy?'

'Don't be ridiculous, Anthony,' Chloë said coldly. 'Dominic is the manager of this hotel.'

'And as such,' Dominic put in coolly, 'I demand, for the second time, to know what is going on here.'

He stood threateningly tall, his expression thunderous.

'For your information,' Anthony replied, indicating Chloë, 'she is my fiancée. She disappeared two days before we were due to get married.'

Dominic turned to Chloë, his dark brows lowered.

'Is this correct?'

Reluctantly, Chloë nodded.

'So that's what all that nonsense about feeling ill was about. You didn't want to come into the dining-room tonight.'

Anthony looked smug.

'So I think you'll understand why I'd like to talk to Chloë, in private.'

'And is this what you want, too, Chloë?'

Chloë thought for a moment. She was loathe to be with Anthony in private but it seemed that, if she refused, he would insist on conducting a slanging match right here in the restaurant.

'OK,' she said slowly. 'Yes. We can go to my room.'

'Very well.' Dominic's tone was curt. 'I think you two had better go and get this sorted out.'

Reluctantly, Chloë watched as Anthony finished his drink, then led him from the restaurant and up to her room.

'Now, let's get this over with. Just say what you want to say, Anthony, and then you can get out of here.'

'Where's the hurry?' he asked, sitting down on the side of her bed.

'I just thought maybe we should talk. After all, you must admit, we have got plenty to talk about.'

Chloë sat down reluctantly on the room's single chair.

'That's better. Now, where were we?' Anthony said.

'I believe we were discussing how you lied to me about your gambling and debts, about why you were out of work, and about why you wanted to marry me,' Chloë reeled off. 'The only reason you wanted to marry me was for my money, and to get a roof over your head. After all, what building society was going to hand out a mortgage to someone with thousands of pounds worth of debts?'

There was a stunned pause.

'All right, maybe some of what you say is true,' Anthony conceded, 'but I wasn't just using you to pay my debts. I did genuinely like you.'

'Like?' Chloë considered the word. 'Yes, maybe you did like me, but is that enough to base a marriage on?'

'I didn't hear you protesting at the time.'

'That's because I believed I was in love with you. But it wasn't the real you. It was an image, a deception, and as soon as I realised that, I fell promptly out of love.'

'Well, maybe once we're marricd you'll come to love me,' he said in a self-pitying tone. 'After all, that's how it works for a lot of couples.'

'You're still under the delusion that I'm actually going to marry you?'

'But why not? We are engaged, after all.'

'Oh, no, we're not! Look, no ring. I threw it out of the train on the way down here.'

'What? That was two hundred and fifty

pounds worth of ring, you know.'

'The last of the big spenders,' Chloë muttered. 'Anyway, haven't you forgotten something? Like the fact that you've got a new girlfriend.'

'Ah, so you heard about that. Actually, Lisa and I are no more.'

'You mean, you've split up already?'

'As soon as I found out where you were,' Anthony announced without batting an eyelid. 'We only got together in the first place because I thought you were never coming back to me.'

'You mean you decided you'd better find some other poor mug to take my place! Only when you saw me in the paper, and read about the rewards I was in line for, you thought perhaps I was a better bet after all.'

Anthony looked so uncomfortable that Chloë knew she must have hit on the truth. Suddenly she realised that she was no longer afraid of him.

'OK,' he said and now had the grace to look sheepish. 'I must admit, the reward was a great enticement to jump on the train, come down here and look for you. Only, now I'm here I realise how much I've missed you.'

He got up off the bed and took a step towards her.

'Haven't you got the message, Anthony?' she said irritably, rising to her feet. 'I'm just not interested.'

'Not interested? You're involved with

110

someone else, is that it? Your sugar daddy downstairs? I knew there was something going on there!'

'Dominic's a far better man than you'll ever be!' Chloë burst out angrily.

'I doubt it. Why don't you just admit that you were only using him to fill in the time till I came to get you back?'

Suddenly Chloë's eyes weren't on Anthony but on a huge black spider on the carpet behind him. She screamed in fear, then the door was suddenly flung open and Dominic stormed in. His eyes flickered over Chloë, whose face was frozen into an expression of horror.

'Just what do you think you're doing to her, you slimy, little—'

Dominic grabbed Anthony by the arm. Chloë wondered if Anthony was going to take a swing at Dominic, then he seemed to lose his balance, stumbling backwards and knocking his head on the bedside cabinet as he staggered to the ground. He tried to get up, but collapsed back on to the floor. At that moment Chloë didn't know why she'd ever feared Anthony. Far from being intimidating, he was merely pathetic, and yet she'd loved him once. She went over to him. There was an angry mark where he'd hit his head, which was already starting to swell. She turned reproachfully to Dominic.

'See what you've done?'

Dominic had stood in silent watchfulness since he'd grabbed Anthony, his fast, angry breathing gradually slowing to normal. Now, however, the anger blazed back into his eyes.

'That drunken rogue was physically assaulting you, and you say I'm in the wrong for pulling him off you?'

'For your information,' Chloë retorted, 'I was perfectly in control of the situation until you came barging in, throwing your weight around!'

'I was not throwing my weight around, Chloë. I heard you screaming. I felt, as manager, that *I* should come to your assistance.'

'I screamed because I saw a spider, not because he was attacking me.'

Dominic's eyes widened in realisation as Chloë went on.

'Talking of coming to my assistance, you did so pretty sharpish. You weren't snooping around outside my door, were you?'

'As a matter of fact, I came upstairs to see if you were OK. I was concerned about you, Chloë,' Dominic said simply. 'And then, as I was about to knock on your door, I heard you scream.'

'So you thought you'd just storm in, and manhandle Anthony?' Chloë shook her head sadly. 'How typical of a man, to see physical violence as the solution to a problem!'

'To my mind, it was the only possible

solution!'

'I think that was up to me to decide, not you. I can run my own life!'

'Fine. I won't interfere any more.'

Dominic strode towards the door, then paused, his hand on the handle.

'I'll leave you in peace with your—your boyfriend, whom, incidentally, you swore did not exist.'

'My private life is my own business,' Chloë retorted.

'That's as may be,' Dominic replied, 'but then, you did volunteer the information. Anyway, I have a hotel to run. And I trust that neither of you will be making a reappearance in the restaurant tonight.'

He went, leaving Chloë feeling emptier than she had ever felt in her life.

CHAPTER EIGHT

Anthony left shortly after Dominic, with a sore head and his train ticket back to Southbridge. Chloë had told him in no uncertain terms that things were over between them because, among other reasons, she was in love with Dominic.

Now, there was nothing to run away from any more. But still, there was no future for her here at the Hotel Collingwood. The sensible thing to do was to see Dominic, and offer her resignation. But as she passed Reception on her way to work the next morning, Linda waylaid her.

'There's a message here for you, Chloë. Looks like the boss's writing.'

Puzzled, Chloë thanked Linda and took the envelope.

'Whatever it's about, looks like you'll get a couple of days' reprieve,' Linda told her.

'Oh? Why's that?'

'Dominic's gone away for a few days. Annual hoteliers' conference in Birmingham. Must be important to make him leave the hotel. He's left Darren in charge. He's got a certificate in hotel management, you know.'

'No, I didn't know.'

'Still, I can't believe Dominic's left this place.'

'Maybe it's a sort of holiday,' Chloë said.

'Holiday? Never! If that man ever married again the only honeymoon he'd take his wife on would be right here, at the Hotel Collingwood.'

Suddenly Linda clapped a hand to her mouth.

'I didn't mean anything by that. After all, I did hear you and he were—'

'Rumours,' Chloë said. 'There's nothing between me and Dominic.'

As soon as she had escaped from Reception, Chloë read the note. In it, Dominic requested to see her on his return from his business trip. It would have been easier to leave now, while he was still away, but perhaps she owed it to him to stay just till then.

With hindsight Chloë wondered if she'd treated him too harshly over the business with Anthony. After all, he had only been trying to help. No, Chloë decided, she'd stay till Dominic got back from his business trip, see him in his office as he wished, and hand in her formal resignation. And she would not go in her disguise, but as her true self.

'You are in demand this morning, Chloë!' Linda's voice assailed her as she passed Reception after finishing work. 'Your friend, Mary Field, has just rung again. Said could you ring her back. D'you want to use this phone?'

'OK, thanks.'

'Oh, hello, Chloë.'

115

Mary's voice sounded unusually excited.

'I've got something to tell you, but I think it might be easier if we discuss things in person. Rob's, got the day off, so he's holding the fort here.'

'Can you come to the hotel? Now? It's OK,' Chloë muttered into the receiver. 'Dominic's away on business.'

'Oh! Right then, I'll see you in the foyer in, say, twenty minutes. That'll give you time to change into your smartest clothes.'

'What? Why?'

'I'll explain when I get there. See you soon.'

'Right,' Chloë agreed reluctantly. 'Oh, and Mary.'

Chloë glanced at Linda, but she was busy with a guest.

'Yes?'

'You might not recognise me,' Chloë said pointedly.

'Oh, I see. Right, I'll look out for a glamorous blonde, dressed in her gladrags. How could I miss you?'

In spite of herself, Chloë laughed as Mary rang off.

'Wow,' Mary breathed later as she walked in through the hotel's revolving doors.

She came up to Chloë, who was sitting on one of the plush sofas in the foyer, flicking through a magazine.

'I told you you wouldn't recognise me,' Chloë muttered, getting to her feet. 'Come on, let's get out of here.'

'I'm afraid you'll have to lose the wig for what I've planned.'

'What? Oh, Mary, you haven't . . . haven't arranged a Press conference about that boy's rescue. Oh, Mary, I'll kill you.'

'Relax,' Mary said, laughing. 'I haven't arranged a Press conference, for goodness' sake, just a brief, informal meeting with the boy's mother, so she can thank you in person.'

Chloë didn't know whether to be thankful or indignant.

'But, Mary, I told you I didn't want any kind of attention drawn to myself.'

'It's all right. She knows you don't want any publicity. We're just going to meet her briefly at her house on the outskirts of the town. You can take the wig off when we arrive, just so she knows it's really you. You know, she's desperate to meet you. I think she really feels she needs to thank you in person, the woman who saved her son's life. So will you do it?'

'Put like that, how can I refuse?'

Charlotte Burrows turned out to be a pleasant, approachable woman with sleek, bobbed hair and a designer navy suit. Her tastefully-furnished house was spectacularly set on the hilly ground to the east of Ecclesdon and after welcoming Chloë and Mary, Charlotte settled them all with a drink in her drawing-room with its breathtaking views of the surrounding countryside.

'Tom, my son, is in Scotland staying with his grandparents for a week or two,' Charlotte explained. 'I thought it best that he got away for a while after what had happened. Otherwise,' she went on, 'I'm sure he'd have liked to have met you again, so that he could have thanked you in person.'

'Oh, well, it really isn't necessary,' Chloë said self-deprecatingly. 'I just did what any other passerby would have done.'

'Maybe,' Charlotte conceded. 'I just thank God that you were there. I would never have forgiven myself if anything had happened to him.'

It was only afterwards in the taxi, when Chloë had tucked her hair back into the wig and Charlotte had gone off to a lunch meeting, that Mary handed her a plain white envelope.

'What's this?' Chloë asked, instantly suspicious.

'It's from Charlotte,' Mary replied. 'She knew you might not take it so she gave it to me.'

Chloë took the envelope. It contained a cheque made out to her, for one thousand pounds. Chloë shoved the envelope back to Mary.

'I don't want it,' she whispered. 'Give it to charity or something.'

Three days later, Dominic waylaid Chloë when she reported for breakfast duty. He didn't meet her eye, merely said, 'Eleven o'clock, my office.'

After work, Chloë showered and changed. Then she put on minimal make-up, and blow-dried her dark hair so that it hung, thick and shiny, to her shoulders. Without the disguise she felt strangely naked as she stepped out of her room, all her old insecurities flocking back to her. But the corridors were quiet, apart from a cleaner too engrossed in her work to look up. Chloë knocked on Dominic's door.

'Come in,' a familiar voice bade her.

So, this was it, the moment of truth.

'Have a seat, Chloë,' Dominic said, without looking up from his paperwork.

'Thank you,' Chloë murmured.

'Now,' Dominic said briskly, looking up. 'I—'

He stopped mid-sentence, his mouth hanging open.

'Chloë,' he breathed, 'It is you, isn't it?'

'Of course it is, Dominic,' Chloë said slowly, suddenly calm. 'You recognise me, don't you?'

'Barely! You've dune something to your hair,' he said, with typical male vagueness. 'Changed it, or something.'

He kept staring.

'I haven't changed it,' Chloë said quietly. 'This is really me, how I have been, all along.'

Suddenly she felt the confidence of the new her coming through.

'You're not making much sense, Chloë.'

'I'll start from the beginning, shall I?'

'I think you'd better,' Dominic said sternly.

119

'Coffee?'

'Yes, please.'

He rose and went over to the percolator as she began.

'My other look, the short, blonde hairstyle, was a wig.'

'A wig?' Dominic frowned. 'But why? I mean, I know women wear these things, for various reasons, but why you, when you're so beautiful anyway?'

His compliment, clearly heartfelt, made Chloë's heart leap.

'I wanted to change my identity, start a new life. So I changed my name from Vale to Johnson, and I changed my looks.'

Dominic's dark eyes narrowed perceptively.

'And what was the reason for this change?'

'I wanted to leave my boyfriend, my fiancé,' she corrected.

'Presumably the same one who came looking for you the other night?'

'Yes.'

'There's just one thing,' Dominic said scrutinising her closely. 'Looking at you now, I keep feeling I've seen you somewhere before.'

'In the national newspapers?' Chloë suggested.

'What?'

'A week or two ago, mystery girl rescues an MP's son from the sea.'

'So that was you?' he asked incredulously.

'I used to go for walks sometimes, without

my disguise, just to get away from it all.'

'You ran away before the police or Press could talk to you because—'

'Because I didn't want my identity to be revealed,' Chloë finished.

'Hang on a minute,' Dominic said. 'I've just remembered where else I recognised you from. It was that time in the Inspiration Point Cafe! I came in, you caught my eye, froze like a frightened rabbit and then bolted.'

'Oh, yes, that time. That's another thing I meant to explain to you. You see, Mary Field and I are friends.'

'You know Mary? But she and her husband are old friends of mine. She never said—'

'That's because I asked her not to,' Chloë explained tentatively. 'You see, she knew me in my real identity, and you knew me in my disguise. I knew that mixing the two up could only be a recipe for disaster.'

Dominic was silent. It was a brooding silence. Then he said, 'Is there anything else you've deceived me about, Chloë? Or perhaps I should phrase that another way. Is there anything you haven't deceived me about?'

'If you mean my feelings for you, then I swear I never deceived you about that. And as for the other things, I never deliberately set out to deceive you or anyone, Dominic.'

'Oh, no?' Dominic sounded severely sceptical. 'It seems to me that you've woven an entire web of lies around yourself, and what for? Just because you wanted to leave your boyfriend?' he said coldly. 'Is that the sort of performance you go through ever time you fancy a change of man?'

'Of course not, Dominic! It's not like that! Let me explain.'

But Dominic wasn't in the mood for listening to explanations.

'I've heard enough,' he silenced her. 'I don't want to listen to any more lies. As far as I'm concerned, you've deceived me from the word go. I'm afraid I've got no other choice than to terminate your employment.'

'You don't need to. I came here today to offer my resignation.'

'So you could run away again?' Dominic asked scornfully.

Chloë's indignation rose.

'I'll tell you why I ran away, shall I? Because my ex-fiancé was an addicted gambler with thousands of pounds' worth of debts. Because I found out he lied to me and used me from day one. Because I was scared of what he and his family would do to me if I told them I didn't want to go ahead with the wedding.'

'He sounds like a charming character, this boyfriend of yours.'

'Ex-boyfriend.' Chloë corrected.

'As far as I'm concerned, when you took his side that night in your room, you chose him. I called you here today to let you know I understood.'

'But you don't understand the situation at all,' Chloë protested.

Dominic's phone rang, right at that moment, cutting her off mid-flow.

'Excuse me.' he told her. 'Dominic Ryan,' he said into the receiver, and after conversing for several seconds he said, 'Hang on a minute.'

He cupped his hand over the receiver.

'Something's come up,' he told Chloë. 'I think we're finished here so if you want to go now—'

'What, go, now? Leave for ever?'

Dominic seemed to relent.

'Why don't you serve out a week's notice first?' he offered, then he turned back to his phone. 'Hello? I do apologise. Now, where were we?'

Slowly, Chloë got up from the chair. As she closed the door behind her, she knew she had never felt more wretched in her life. So this, she realised numbly, was what it felt like when your heart was breaking.

Later that afternoon, she called in on Mary at the café.

'So, I told him the whole sorry story,' Chloë said miserably to her friend. 'And, he ended up sacking me,' Chloë blurted out.

'Oh, Chloë, I'm sorry! I mean, I'm sorry Dominic took it like that.'

'I suppose I can't blame Dominic,' Chloë went on. 'He was right. I had deceived him, from the start. I guess that when you're having a relationship with someone, you take it as read that they're being honest with you. I don't think he'll ever forgive me.'

'I wouldn't be so sure,' Mary said consolingly. 'I know Dominic can fly off the handle, but he's not the sort to bear a grudge.'

'Not that it'll make much difference to me,' Chloë said gloomily. 'I'm serving out a week's notice, then I'll be out of his life for ever.'

'And what about you?' Mary asked. 'Do you still feel the same about him? Do you still love him?'

'Of course I do. I suppose that's just a cross I'll have to bear.'

'Chloë! Don't be so defeatist. Are you just going to give up now?'

'I don't see that I have any choice.'

'You could try to win him back,' Mary suggested.

'Oh, Mary, you sound like a women's magazine! And besides, I'm not at all sure he wants to be won back,' Chloë added honestly. 'I've probably destroyed any feelings he might once have had for me.'

'Nonsense, Chloë,' Mary said briskly. 'Dominic must still have some feelings for you, to have got so upset when you confessed everything.'

'I wish I could be as confident as you,' Chloë said doubtfully. 'He wouldn't even listen to me when I tried to explain.'

'Yes, well, I know Dominic can be stubborn sometimes,' Mary conceded. 'But I think I've got an idea about how you can offer him the olive branch, if you want to hear it.'

'Go on then.' Chloë sighed. 'Apart from the remains of my dignity, what have I got to lose?'

*   *   *

'Hi there, Chloë, how's it going?'

Chloë turned, to see Darren coming in through the kitchen's swing doors.

'Oh, hi, fine thanks. Oh, Darren, I wanted to have a word with you.'

'That's funny, because I wanted to have a word with you, too.'

Darren looked distinctly uneasy.

'I'm not sure how to say this, but the thing is, Chloë, well, I've met a girl.'

'That's great news,' Chloë said impetuously. 'I'm really pleased for you. So, tell me all about her.'

'What is there to say?' Darren grinned. 'I met her in the nightclub last weekend. She's called Anna, she's nineteen, and she's gorgeous!'

Chloë smiled at his enthusiasm.

'Anyway, what was it you wanted to talk to me about?' he asked.

'Well,' Chloë began, 'it's more of a favour, actually.'

'Mary, are you sure this is going to work?' Chloë asked nervously as she sat in the empty café.

'It'll work,' Mary said soothingly. 'Trust me.'

'I feel a bit over-dressed,' Chloë complained, glancing down at the little black dress Mary had insisted she buy.

'Nonsense. You look stunning,' Mary said briskly. 'And you can't say I haven't made an effort to improve the atmosphere of your surroundings.'

Chloë glanced at the single red rose Mary had placed in the small vase on the table next to the white envelope that lay there, and smiled.

'Thanks for everything,' she told Mary, 'whatever the outcome of this crazy scheme.'

'I suppose I might as well go upstairs,' Mary said. 'He should be here any minute.'

'Oh, Mary, don't go.' Chloë grimaced nervously. 'You can't leave me.'

'You'll be fine,' Mary said firmly, getting up. 'And besides, I've got no desire to play gooseberry. I'd wish you luck, but I'm sure you won't need it, looking like that.'

Almost as soon as she had gone, there was a noise at the cafeteria door and someone entered.

'Chloë?'

Dominic frowned, obviously surprised to see

her.

He was dressed smartly but casually, hair windswept back from his face.

'What are you doing here?'

His dark eyes ran over her, taking in the short black dress with its scooped neckline, Chloë's shining dark brown hair, sparkling green eyes and keyed-up, glowing complexion.

'I came here to see Mary. She wanted to speak to me about a business proposition.'

'Just a ruse to get you here, I'm afraid,' Chloë confessed, flushing slightly. 'You see, I wanted to talk to you.'

Dominic looked surprised for a moment, then his face set into a frown.

'Well, what was it you wanted to say?'

Chloë sighed. This wasn't going to be easy.

'Aren't you going to sit down?' she challenged him.

For a moment she thought Dominic was going to refuse, but then he pulled out the old wooden chair opposite hers.

'Well?' he barked.

Silently, Chloë slid the envelope across the table towards him.

'What's this?' he asked warily.

'Open it and find out,' she suggested.

Dominic glanced at her, eyes narrowed suspiciously, as he picked up the envelope and slipped out the flap. Slowly he slid out the slips of paper inside, studying them in silence for a few moments.

'What do I want with a fortnight's holiday in Rhodes, flying out tomorrow?'

His voice was ominously toneless.

'I thought that maybe we could go together. It's my way of making it up to you for the things I've done.'

'Chloë,' Dominic said slowly, in a cold, controlled voice, 'I don't know if it has escaped your notice, but I have a hotel to run. How did you propose I did that while umpteen thousand miles away in the Greek islands?'

'I've taken care of all that,' Chloë replied calmly. 'I've had a word with Darren, and he's more than happy to stand in for you while you're away.'

'You've been discussing the running of my hotel with Darren Andrews?' Dominic exploded. 'You've been discussing this crackpot scheme, not to mention our relationship, with Andrews?'

'I didn't mention anything personal.'

Chloë struggled to retain control of her own temper.

'I just told him that you might be going away soon for a couple of weeks. He did seem a bit puzzled that I was asking him, but he didn't ask any awkward questions.'

'And what made you think Andrews was qualified to run the Hotel Collingwood?' Dominic fumed.

'The fact that he's got a diploma in hotel management,' Chloë suggested, 'and the fact

128

that you trusted him enough to leave him in charge when you went away the other week.'

'A couple of nights is an entirely different matter to a whole fortnight!'

Dominic scraped his chair back, getting to his feet.

'And I don't need you or anyone else telling me how to run my hotel.'

He stomped towards the door.

'I take it that's a no then?' Chloë asked in a small voice.

'You're damned right!'

And he was gone, leaving the door banging after him. Chloë slumped in her chair, head in her hands. She'd never felt so humiliated, so rejected in her life. She'd known it wouldn't work. Why, oh, why had she let Mary talk her into it? Now that it had all gone so spectacularly wrong, her first instinct was to find her friend, to ask what to do now. But Mary, of course, was tucked away upstairs, with her husband and children. No, Chloë was on her own this time. If there was anything to be salvaged from this situation, it was up to her to do it.

She got to her feet, racing to the door. If she ran she just might catch Dominic before he left the carpark. As she emerged from the café into the evening air, she saw Dominic, standing near the edge of the cliff. He must have been so deep in his thoughts that he didn't hear her approach on the grass. Chloë's instinct was to reach out and touch him, but she was afraid of making him jump, possibly over the edge of the cliff. She almost said his name, but decided this might have a similar effect. So she simply gave a low, discreet cough. Dominic spun round.

'Oh, it's you,' he muttered.

'Dominic,' Chloë pleaded, taking a step nearer, 'we have to talk. I can't leave with things the way they are between us.'

'There's nothing to talk about,' Dominic said in a flat voice. 'As far as I'm concerned it's over. If you think you can make everything all right by waving some airline tickets at me like a magic wand, then I'm afraid you've got another think coming.'

'Of course I know I can't make everything all right that easily. I know now that I've messed you about, practically since we first got involved with each other. You see, the thing was, I just couldn't let myself believe I could trust you. There were problems, in my past. I'd been hurt before, by Anthony.'

'Ah, yes, Anthony,' Dominic echoed tonelessly. 'And where does he come into all of this?'

'I tried to tell you before. Anthony means nothing to me now. I sent him back to Southbridge.'

'But whatever gave you the idea that you could repair things between us by springing some holiday on me out of the blue?' Dominic

130

asked irritably.

Chloë decided she might as well come clean.

'It was Mary's idea. This whole little scheme was Mary's idea. She knew I didn't want to accept the reward money for the boy I saved, so she suggested I bought these holiday tickets with it instead. I wasn't keen, but she said it was worth a try. She had some hunch that you cared for me.'

Dominic turned to her.

'But of course I love you, Chloë,' he said quietly, 'that's what makes this all so painful.'

'What?' Chloë breathed, scarcely believing her ears.

'Naturally, at first I tried to deny it to myself,' Dominic went on. 'Because you weren't my type, my usual type, I should say. But it was no good. It wasn't long before I had to admit the truth, and it was then I realised I might as well stop fighting it.'

Chloë's heart had leaped while he was talking, and now it pounded rapidly as she replied.

'Well, then, if you love me, and I've apologised for the way I've behaved in the past, can't we give it one more try?'

There was a silence.

'You'll do anything to get me to go on holiday,' Dominic growled eventually.

'Forget the holiday!' Chloë burst out. 'I don't care about that. All I care about is you.'

'You care about me?' Dominic asked slowly, warily. 'What exactly do you mean by that?'

'That I love you, of course!' Chloë said exasperatedly.

For the first time, she thought she saw the tension lift from Dominic's face. It was as if he'd noticed her properly for the first time.

'Hey, aren't you cold in that excuse for a dress?' he asked.

'Mary assured me that you'd be bowled over by it—the dress, that is,' Chloë told him, shivering slightly.

Then, not needing any further invitation, Dominic pulled her roughly into his arms and kissed her with passionate urgency. They'd been apart for too long, Chloë realised as she responded eagerly. When they eventually drew apart, Dominic retained her within the warmth of his arms.

'You'd better not kiss me again,' he warned breathlessly as his eyes drank her in. 'This is hardly the time or the place.'

He glanced around him at the wind-ruffled clifftop.

'So I can tell Mary the dress was a success after all?' Chloë asked.

'The dress is irresistible,' Dominic told her, pulling her close again. 'And as for you, you're gorgeous, more gorgeous than I could ever have imagined. Come on,' Dominic commanded. 'Let's go in and tell that scheming Mary Field that her plan worked out after all.'

'Apart from the holiday.'

'Oh, maybe that isn't such a bad idea after all.'

'What?' Chloë turned to him. 'But you seemed so cross!'

'Yes, I was, wasn't I? Are you really sure you want to take on someone like me?'

'Sure, and I don't blame you for reacting the way you did. I expect it was a shock, that's all.'

'It was a shock. I'm not used to people caring about me.'

'Well, you've got me to care about you now. You'd better get used to it!'

'I think I could learn to live with it,' Dominic replied as they neared the café. 'And I'll always be there for you, too. When I think how scared and alone you must have been all your life.'

'Let's not think about that now,' Chloë urged him, moving closer. 'As you say, I've got you now.'

A sudden thought occurred to Dominic.

'Of course, you'll have to reveal your true identity to the others at the hotel.'

'I know. I think I'll just tell everyone I've got a new hairstyle.'

She ran her fingers through her long dark hair.

'This could do with a cut anyway. And besides, I'll feel happier when I'm no longer living a lie.'

'Me, too,' Dominic concurred. 'There's one condition to me coming on this holiday with you, though.'

'What's that?'

'That you marry me while we're away.'

'It's a deal,' Chloë said in relief and joy.

'Great. You know what this means?' Dominic asked, smiling, too.

'No. What?'

'That from now on you'll be barefoot and pregnant in the kitchen.'

'Now why isn't that such an appalling prospect as it should be?' Chloë mused aloud, before Dominic silenced her once more with a kiss.

We hope you have enjoyed this Large Print book. Other Chivers Press or G.K. Hall & Co. Large Print books are available at your library or directly from the publishers.

For more information about current and forthcoming titles, please call or write, without obligation, to:

Chivers Press Limited
Windsor Bridge Road
Bath BA2 3AX
England
Tel. (01225) 335336

OR

G.K. Hall & Co.
P.O. Box 159
Thorndike, Maine 04986
USA
Tel. (800) 223-2336

All our Large Print titles are designed for easy reading, and all our books are made to last.